A TAIL OF TWO KITTIES
A Reverse Harem Tail

The Fox and the Hounds, book 2

by

Jacquelyn Faye

A TAIL OF TWO KITTIES
A Reverse Harem Tail

Fox and the Hounds, book 2

ISBN: 978-1-945893-11-7

Published by Untold Press LLC
114 NE Estia Lane
Port St Lucie, FL 34983

www.untoldpress.com

PRODUCED IN THE UNITED STATES OF AMERICA

10 9 8 7 6 5 4 3 2 1

Dedication

Don't know if anybody has done this before, but I hereby dedicate this book to my main character,

Kaede Motherfuckin' Tanaka

I FLOVE you, you sassy little bitch.

And I want to apologize for all the shit I put you through in this book.

Don't hate me.

Chapter 1

"Ert werz the berst of terms, ert werz the werst of terms..."

"What the fuck is she saying?" Rome gave Hiroki a pleading look.

"I believe that one was, it was the best of times, it was the worst of times, Rome-*sama*."

"See?" I twirled around the lamp post in the village. "Hiroki gets me."

"Why is it the worst of times, Kaede-*sama*?"

"Berkerz." I stopped spinning around the ancient green iron post and frowned at the two of them. "This was fun, but it would have been a lot more fun if Remy and David could have come, too."

It was Saturday night, and I'd been annoying *everybody* in the common room of Breckenridge Hall. In an effort to spare my hide, Rome and Hiroki had grabbed me and practically dragged me to the village to burn off some energy. The grateful looks of the students trying to relax kind of hurt my feel badz, so I'd reluctantly agreed.

Remy, Rome's twin and my boyfriend extraordinaire, had been saddled with guard duty at the Temple of Doom. It was more of a cavern, but it still housed the spirit of the Norse god, Fenrir. So, Temple of Doom kind of fit. Only it wasn't our doom as the old stories went. It was Asgard's.

Fenrir had a *huuuge* grudge against the Aesir branch of the Norse pantheon. Not that I could blame him. They had bound him in chains, trapped his spirit in a cave, and his body in Hell. I would have been pissed off, too. And I'm sure if my parents could have managed a similar punishment for me, my happy ass would have been right there alongside him. Instead, they shipped me off to boarding school to learn to act more human.

Putting an Inari fox, a celestial messenger for the gods, that close to the sleeping wolf god had been the biggest mistake of their lives. I'd become his herald after he metaphysically stole me from the Inari-*kami*. He tells me on a regular basis that it is my destiny to awaken him, reunite his body and soul, and unleash him upon the Aesir gods of Asgard.

Sounded like a dick move to me. I was happy spending time with my three-and-a-half boyfriends. Shooting Rome a nervous glance, I got the familiar tingle in my stomach. He was the half a boyfriend. We were more than friends but were taking it slow. Just friends didn't kiss each other with tongue. Semantics aside, I had no intention of unleashing Fenrir on Asgard. I'm sure that would have broken every leash law on the books, and I didn't need a bunch of pissed off gods coming after me with spears and lightning hammers.

Except maybe Thor. He could cum after me. After he made me cum with his mighty hammer… I mean, it was only fair.

As for David, he was still in the infirmary. When he'd been kidnapped, his ex-girlfriend had spelled him, or drugged him, unconscious. He was awake, but still not up to normal. The school nurse refused to let him leave the infirmary until he showed signs of improvement, and the twins' sister, Sabine, wasn't talking to anybody. Not that the average student would accidentally run into her any time soon, seeing as she was locked in the school dungeon. Yes, our school had a dungeon. No, I hadn't gotten my smart ass locked up, yet. Stay tuned.

"So, where are you two hunka hunka burnin' loves taking me?"

"To a psychiatrist," Rome mumbled under his breath.

8

I poked him in the side, right between his ribs. "Fox ears, remember?"

He yelped and grabbed my finger in his massive hand, pulling it from his tickle spot and giving me a death glare. He was scary, when he wasn't being so fucking sexy. Just friends didn't drool over chiseled jaws and shoulder-length blond hair. Nor did they suffer from wet panties just from piercing gazes. I needed to learn to control my piercing gazes. Rome was grumpy when his panties got wet. Grumpier.

Hiroki's foxlike hissing laughter permeated the night air. I poked him with my other hand, forgetting he wasn't ticklish in the least. It was one of the most un-fun parts of Hiroki. The rest of his parts were a *lot* of fun. Especially the long, pointy ones.

"Are you hungry?" Rome's voice slithered through my auditory canals and caressed the pleasure sensors of my brain. I nodded.

"Kaede-*sama* is *always* hungry."

"Then we should get some food into her before she has any liquor."

"That's two of the three major food groups." I nodded sagely.

"What's the third?" Rome sounded afraid to ask.

"Dick." I grinned at him, pumping my fist as he rolled his eyes.

"In that order?" Hiroki snickered.

"Of course! Dick always comes after you liquor. Get it? Liquor…lick her?"

"Yes, Kaede-*sama*. I got it." He shook his head, but I could see the small tugging of a smile on his lips.

Rome just looked like he wanted to go back to school and forget the whole night had ever been his idea. "Lady Hel, help me get through this night," he said exasperatedly.

I slapped his arm and made a shushing motion with my finger, glaring at him piercingly. He deserved wet panties after bringing up that bitch's name. She was the goddess his people, hellhounds, revered. She'd created them, after all.

We were out to have a good time, and I didn't need his accidental invocation getting her all up in my business.

"Sorry," he whispered.

"If I'm forbidden from mentioning the F-word, you're not allowed to say her name, either. We are ignoring the problem until it goes away."

"I am confused. You say the F-word on an average of two-point-five times a sentence." Hiroki scrunched his eyebrows.

"Not that one. The one that ends in enrir."

"Oh. *Hai*."

I stood on my tiptoes and patted his head.

"Come on. I'm hungry, too," Rome grumbled and headed in a familiar direction.

"Oooh, are we going to the pub?"

"Yes."

"Not eating any pickled testicles or fermented shark nuggets. Just warning you in advance... Nor do I want to get knocked unconscious in the bathroom or thrown over the side of a boat in the middle of the ocean." I frowned at Rome's back. "Can we go somewhere else? Place is kind of dangerous in hindsight."

Rome stopped walking and turned around, seemingly lost in thought. It was uncharted territory for him, and I couldn't blame him for getting lost. "The number of restaurants is limited in Oddi, but I know another place you might like."

He was being nice, again. I shuddered in pleasure, liking the unusual feeling.

We still walked through the central square, but instead of going straight, Rome turned onto the only other major street that ran through the village. Gasping, I stopped walking and stared in adoration at the very familiar red and white marquee.

"They have KFC. In Iceland? In the village?"

"Yes. There is a McDonald's, too," Rome said over his shoulder.

The closer we got, my mouth started watering as the comforting smell wafted over us. "Roki, chicken."

He nodded, just as mesmerized as I was. "*Hai*."

Foxes just loved them some chicken. Even when it was deep fried. Who am I trying to kid? *Especially* when it was deep fried. Deep frying made *everything* better. "I'ma get a bucket of cheekin."

Rome stopped, his hand on the door. "Do you want to go somewhere else?"

"No!" Roki's voice matched mine in pitch *and* intensity as we said it together.

"Oh. Just thought you might want to go someplace a little nicer that serves alcohol."

"Food, *then* liquor."

"Okay," he said defensively and opened the door.

I inhaled deeply as soon as we were inside, closing my eyes, and letting the happies warm my tummy. "Mmmm. Smells like home. Without all the pollution and patchouli."

If there was one thing I hated about northern California, it was the smell of patchouli wafting from the more free-spirited of the human population. That and Axe Body Spray. It was almost overwhelming to a human nose. To a fox nose, it was torture.

As soon as I looked up at the oh, so familiar menu, I cringed in guilt. It was in Icelandic, but that wasn't the issue. Roki and I didn't have any funds available. My parents had shipped us off with two gold coins to pay our cab fare, and that was it.

"What's the matter?" Rome bumped me with his shoulder after I'd stopped moving.

I growled in frustration. *Hating* the fact that he, once again, would have to pay for our meal. "I'm sorry we don't have any money, Rome."

"I would not have abducted you if I were worried about that."

Roki poked me in the side and grinned.

"What?"

He pulled out a black credit card from his front pocket and gave me a wink. "We are no longer poor."

"Where the fuck did you get that?" I tried to snatch it out of his hand, but it was like trying to snatch a playing card from a magician.

"I wrote your mother. Told her of our predicament. She sent it with express instructions not to let you get your grubby little paws on it, use it to buy alcohol, and set the school ablaze."

I stopped reaching, *wanting* so bad to argue on behalf of myself, but who was I kidding? My mother was right. "Okay."

He blinked in surprise. "You are fine with this?"

"Maybe. We'll play a game. *If* I can steal it or get my hands on it, I get drunk, and the school gets toasted. In the *meantime,* you can be my personal banker."

"I accept your terms," he answered with a grin and stuffed the card back into his pocket. "Dinner is our treat tonight, Rome-*sama*."

"Thank you."

Apparently, in Iceland, it is almost shocking to order three buckets of chicken for three people. The poor teenage girl working the register did a triple take. One for each bucket of chicken, and then asked three times if we were sure.

"Oh, and three large Cokes," I added just a few seconds before she swiped the card.

She stopped, mid motion, gave me a look of pure exasperation, punched a few buttons, swiped the card, and handed it back to Hiroki. Even though I was holding out my grubby little paw.

I stuck my tongue out at her as I grabbed one of the trays and headed for a cozy little corner booth in the back, sliding into the middle. "Bet she's fun at parties."

Rome laughed as he slid in beside me. Roki blocked me in on the other, effectively making a Kaede sammich. I was good with that and pressed my face to each of their shoulders, happy in the moment.

"Does she always get like this before she eats?"

"Worse, after," Hiroki answered Rome.

He sighed and tore the cardboard lid out of the bucket, grabbing the piece on top and tearing a hunk of flesh out of it. I had a drumstick in my hand when I stopped and looked at Hiroki. "I'll have four fried chickens and a Coke…"

His eyes squinted as he grinned at me, getting my reference. Roki was a lot older than me, how much I wasn't sure. Strangely enough, one of his favorite movies of all times was Blues Brothers.

"I don't get it," Rome said, watching our exchange.

"It's from a movie."

"Oh." He swallowed some of his Coke, washing the chicken down and putting the bones on the lid.

"Did you suck the meat off?" I stared at the bone. There wasn't a sliver of meat left on it.

"My name isn't Kaede." He smirked, sooo proud of himself.

"Not gonna argue." I popped the chicken leg into my mouth and pulled off nearly all of the meat, glaring at him as I dropped the bone next to his.

"Holy shit."

"I have nimble lips."

"She does," Hiroki said with a nod.

Rome just stared, blushed, and fished out another piece of chicken.

The rest of dinner was wolfed down in almost a contest like fashion. I tapped out with two pieces left, leaning back in the booth and rubbing my tummy happily while Roki and Rome finished theirs. And then fought over my last two pieces.

To eat again… The whispered thought in my mind sent a shiver down my spine. Fenrir was hungry. I could hear it in his voice. Not wanting to alert the other two with me, I schooled my face, not daring to change my expression.

They had KFC back then?

I do not know of which you speak. But fowl… That was certainly in abundance. I can still feel the hot blood

13

against my tongue as their bones snapped between my jaws.

You should go mouse hunting with Roki when you wake up. He likes mooshi. I used my made-up word for mouse sushi.

Mice? I could devour all the rodents in the world and not be satisfied.

And you'd probably piss Roki off.

I care not.

Why? Roki's sweet, and if he didn't have any more mice, he'd be sad.

Very well. I shall feast upon cattle and leave the rodents to him.

I'll let him know.

Find my body, my fox. Find it so I may be whole again.

Just like *that*, he was gone from my mind, and Roki and Rome were staring at me worriedly again. "What?"

"Fenrir," they said in unison.

Sighing, I nodded. I sucked at schooling my face. I shouldn't have been surprised, I generally sucked at school in general. And all things school related. Except school shopping. That, I loved. New things made me smile.

"Yeah. He wants some cheekin, too."

"He hungers for things mortal," Rome said worriedly.

"And he wants me to find his body."

"You cannot!"

"No shit, Sherznola." I motioned for him to let me out of the booth. "I gotta pee."

Roki was quicker with the booty slide and held out his hand to help me. Unfortunately, I was wearing a skirt, and the sound my legs made being dragged across the plastic bench made everybody wince. "Uh… Ow!"

"I am sorry, Kaede-*sama*!"

I rubbed my ass as I stood, giving him a small pout. "You can kiss it better later."

"With pleasure," he answered and bowed.

"There better be!" I swatted him in the stomach as he stood up, satisfied with the little *oomph* he made.

14

Grabbing the handle of the bathroom door, I pulled it open and took one step closer to Hell. That wasn't a jab at the cleanliness of the restroom, either. I'd been there once and instantly recognized it by sight, smell, and that warm dry heat you just can't quite get anywhere else. Someone had turned the Colonel's lavatory into a portal to the underworld. "That's some shitty southern hospitality," I whispered and closed the door before I turned around and walked back to the table. "On second thought, I'll pee at the club."

You will find my body…

Like hell, I will, I thought to myself, praying Fenrir couldn't hear me.

∞ ∞ ∞

"You have garnered more admirers, Kaede-*sama*."

I blinked up at Roki. He had barely whispered, but I'd heard him as clear as day, even over the throbbing club music. "What? Where?"

He began turning to the music, giving me the opportunity to face the direction he had been. "The two at the table, wearing similar clothing. They have been staring at you since we entered."

They looked a *lot* alike, but not identical. They *might* have been brothers, or cousins, or in the same fraternity, but they weren't twins. Thankfully. Dealing with one set was more than enough to handle. Especially with Rome. We'd gone clubbing and he was too proud to dance with me at the same time as Roki, so we'd been alternating all night. Just when things started getting fun with either of them, it was time to switch.

The two at the table both wore jeans and button-down shirts of differing colors, but oddly enough, they were still coordinated. One had a gray shirt with bluish hair in a short-cropped ponytail. The other had gray hair with a bluish shirt but was going for the messy bed-head look. They were both really fucking hot, but totally gay. They set

15

off my gaydar as soon as my eyes settled on their chiseled good looks and matching ensembles. No wonder Roki had honed -in on them. "Think they're staring at you, buddy. You might be more their type."

"I thought so at first, too. But when I accidentally ran my hand over your buttocks, lifting your skirt, it was you they were staring at."

"Wait. You used me as bait?"

"I often use you to bate in some capacity," he said with his fox snicker.

Roki made a lewd joke. I was so fucking proud, I stood on my toes and kissed him in the middle of the dance floor.

"You are going to drive away your new suitors," he said in shock after I pulled away.

"Not interested. I have more than enough. Besides," I said, slapping him on the arm, "we're dating. You're supposed to get all jealous and shit, not show people my butt."

"Chances are, you would have exposed it sooner or later. I was expediting the process."

"True story." I nodded for emphasis. "But still no jelly? I'm hurt."

"You wish me to be jealous of your admirers? Your boyfriends?"

"No, and yes. Kinda. I don't know. You're supposed to want me all for yourself. David and them are pack. I get that."

He pulled me close and pressed his lips to my ear, kissing it gently before whispering. "There is more of you than I can handle. Something as grand as you is meant to be shared. Not hoarded."

"You think I'm a hoard," I joked, intentionally softening the D sound.

"A sexy little hoard."

"You just like playing with the other guys." I slapped his chest lightly.

"*Hai*. That, too." He winked. "Are they still watching you?" A hint of a smile turned up the corners of his lips in a way that never failed to mesmerize me. I didn't want to tear my gaze from his beautiful smile, not even to answer his question.

"I don't care, Roki."

His smile got even bigger, and my heart melted a little more as he spun me around the dance floor. When I finally did look back to the table, the two guys were gone.

"See. I told you they weren't interested."

"They probably saw me gazing at your beauty and gave up."

That earned him another kiss.

"Let's go home."

"Will you settle for school?"

"Wherever *you* are. That's home."

Chapter 2

The wet towel I'd wrapped around my hair slapped against my back as I stood up. Grabbing my bathrobe off the hook of the shower stall, I groaned as the mead-induced headache I'd earned from over drinking the night before threatened to squeeze the eyeballs from my tiny little head.

"I need to quit drinking so much," I groaned, and then laughed at the absurdity of my statement.

It was Saturday morning. More like early afternoonish, but that was the joy of the weekends. No classes. Even Hiroki was still sleeping when I'd dragged my ass out of bed, sniffed my pits, and decided a shower was very much needed after a long night of drinking and dancing. The shower had done the trick, but I was going to need to get dressed and get some food into me to get rid of the headache and face the rest of the world.

I stuffed my shower things into the plastic-coated canvas bag Hiroki had procured for me somewhere and stepped out of the shower stall, nearly slipping on the wet tile. "Woah."

I was a still little unsteady on my feet, too. Food was definitely the first thing on the agenda after clothes. The rest of the day was still a complete mystery to me, but at least I had a place to start.

The hallway was starting to get a little crowded, and I should have had to weave my way through the other students, but wherever I walked, they parted and gave me a very wide birth. Almost as if they were afraid to touch me. It was unsettling, to say the least. Unconsciously, I sniffed my pits again through my wet terrycloth robe, but all I could smell was my floral body wash. Ignoring everyone and everything around me, I plodded to my room, keeping my eyes focused on the carpet ahead of me. I could still feel their stares as I shoved the key into the lock, and by the time I finally got the door opened and into the room, I was breathing almost frantically.

"Kaede-*sama*? Are you all right?"

Roki's worried tone brought me back to reality. "Yeah. I'm fine, why?" I lied and tried to sound as normal as possible.

"Because I can hear you gasping for breath from here." He got up off his bed and peeked around the corner at me.

I realized I was clutching my chest and let go, nodding and walking into the room confidently. "Just a minor panic attack." I opted for the truth, already having been busted for lying once.

"Again, I ask. Is everything all right?"

I tossed my stuff on the end of my bed and nodded. "Weirdest thing. The hallway was kind of packed. It felt like everybody was staring and avoiding me. It kind of set me on edge."

He nodded and walked over to me, wrapping me in his muscular arms and kissing the top of my head. "You are safe."

"In your arms? Always." I pressed my face against his equally muscular chest. He had gone to bed in his boxers and nothing else. I smiled as my cheek heated against his skin, and I breathed in his scent. Even after a night of partying, he still smelled delicious. "I'm hungry. Let's go get some food."

"*Hai.*" He let go and stepped back, eyeing me appraisingly. I must have passed whatever visual scrutiny he had subjected me to, and he turned, pulling out a pair of clean uniform pants from the dresser.

I dropped my robe from my shoulders and did the same, smiling to myself as I caught Roki casting sidelong glances at my nakedness. "Get a good look, perv?"

"*Hai,* Kaede-*sama.*" He snickered.

I turned my butt toward him and bent over exaggeratedly to get a skirt out of the bottom drawer. He hissed as he breathed in. Glancing over my shoulder, I gave him an embarrassed look. "Don't look at me there. It is embarrassing…"

"As if you could be."

I laughed and wiggled my butt at him, grabbing the skirt. Before I could stand up, he struck, slapping the left cheek of my ass. I yelped and laughed, running away from him to get dressed. Food first, sex later. A girl has to have priorities, and my stomach was more awake than my foxy bits, but they weren't too far behind.

"Ready?" I asked after I slipped on my school issued, plain blazer.

"*Hai.*" He took my hand and led me to the door, only pausing to open it for me and usher me though. He locked up behind us, and we headed for the dining hall. "You are hungry." He didn't ask, he made a statement.

"Staaarving."

"I can tell."

"How?"

"You are practically running."

I slowed down, almost tripping after I realized he was struggling to keep up. Hiroki wasn't the tallest of men, but his legs were longer than mine. I must have looked like a blurry white streak to anybody seeing us pass by. "Sorry."

He chuckled. "Do not be."

I grabbed his hand and let him set the pace after that.

Luckily, we had missed the lunch rush, and the dining hall was mostly empty. Unfortunately, that meant the selection of food had dwindled down. Not the quantity, just the variety. That didn't stop me from filling my plate with roasted chicken, mashed taters, and a heaping helping of buttered corn. That would be a good start to filling the ravenous hole that had become my belly. I even grabbed a side salad.

We set our trays down, and I turned to go get something to drink, but Roki stopped me with an outstretched hand. "Tea or soda?"

"Sweet iced tea, please."

"*Hai.*"

I smiled at his retreating back and sat down at the worn wood table, grabbing my utensils and groaning a little as the first bite of chicken hit my tongue.

"Is this seat taken?"

Looking up, I smiled at the twin standing over our table. "Actually, yes. Let's grab a bigger table. I figured you guys ate already."

Rome or Remy turned and set his tray down on the table beside us, large enough for four people, and grabbed mine just as I'd set my silverware down. I stood and grabbed Roki's, setting it down across from me.

"I would have grabbed it," the twin answered. It was getting more and more frustrating that I couldn't tell them apart. I didn't know whether to kiss him on the lips, or kiss him on the lips with tongue and grab his ass.

"It's not like Roki eats like me," I answered, pointing at the barely filled plate.

"Nobody eats like you."

"Awww. You're so sweet," I said and slapped him gently on the back of the head as I sat and picked my fork back up to shovel more food in my mouth.

Romy, as I was starting to refer to them in my head until I could nonchalantly figure out which one I was talking to, laughed and picked up a chicken leg, tearing a piece out of it. "Don't feel bad. We eat more than David, too. Think it has to do with how much magic we burn."

"I don't feel bad. I feel hungry."

Romy chuckled and took another bite just as Roki came back with drinks. "Greetings, Remy-*san.*"

Remy! I should have grabbed his ass and slipped him some tongue. It's not like Rome would have complained, anyway. I turned to Roki and stared at him blankly. "Wait. *You* can tell them apart? How?"

He just winked at me and touched his finger to the side of his nose.

Damn you and your sniffer. Roki was a *nogitsune*, a distant relation to the *kitsune*. They weren't as spiritually or magically powerful as *kitsune*, but were more akin to their fox selves in human form, and we were no match for them physically.

I leaned in a little closer to Remy and took a whiff. He smelled good, damn good, but I couldn't tell a difference between him and Rome. "Do I stink?"

"No. You smell good. But could I talk you into wearing a different cologne than your brother?"

"And make your life easier? I don't think so."

"You like that I can't tell you apart anymore."

"I do."

"You're evil."

"Hellhound, remember?"

I pouted and took another bite of my chicken, daintily using a utensil instead of picking up the whole damn thing like I wanted and shoving it in my face. KFC, the night before, was more like it. Not like you could eat chicken with a spork. They encouraged barbarism.

Roki sat down and started in on his food, too. It was fun watching him fumble with a fork, and I smiled and did the same when he gave up and tore pieces of his chicken off and ate them with his fingers. "So, what are *you* up to today?" I stopped eating long enough to look over at Remy.

"Going to check on David."

"Can I come with you?"

"I'm sure he'd like that."

I frowned at my food, feeling a little guilty for not already having plans to do just that. Horrible girlfriend was my middle name, though.

"Don't worry. He's doing fine. The school nurse just doesn't want him overdoing it."

Nodding, I picked at my food instead of eating it.

The other two must have picked up on my mood, and the three of us ate in silence. Until an explosion rocked the ground beneath our feet. Our plates rattled, and a few of the other students screamed as they ducked beneath the table. Roki stood, but didn't move, immediately signifying we weren't in any immediate danger.

"What the hell happened?" I watched his face as Roki tilted his head and stared toward the exit.

"An explosion."

"No shit, Shirleylocks. Where?"

"Not close. The main building perhaps?"

"That's not where the Home Economics class is…"

They both stared at me.

"What?"

"Not every explosion has to do with your cooking, Kaede-*sama*."

"I know. That only happened once, but the kitchen is the only place where there is gas and open flame. I know because I checked. There's nothing in the main building that is explosive. Unless Uncle Tatsuo farted."

"No…" Remy stood up and slowly turned toward the exit.

"What?"

"The dungeon…" He took off running without looking back.

"His sister sploded?" I shot Roki a confused glance.

Understanding dawned on his face. I could see it.

"What?"

"No. But an explosion would free her from imprisonment…"

"Ohhh. Okay. Wait, what?"

Roki took off running. I grabbed a chicken leg and ran after him. Don't judge, I nervous eat. Happy eat, sometimes sad eat. Definitely horny eat. Oh, and I could enter a competition when I angry eat. Angry eating is the best. It's right up there with angry sex.

As soon as I got outside, I froze with the chicken leg in my mouth, staring at the castle that was the main hall of Aesir Academy. At the base of the building, a billowing cloud of smoke poured from a hole that hadn't been there when we went to lunch.

Several professors were gasping for air around the brand-new entrance and doing what they could with water magics to douse the flames that had spread to the grass and bushes around the area. I was pretty far away, but I could still make out Remy as he plowed through the gathering crowd and vanished into the dark hole. Worry filled me as I watched him disappear, and then Roki followed him, and my worry turned to panic.

Bad Roki! I spat out the chicken and ran after them.

The smoke instantly burned my nose as I ducked through the students milling about, gawking at the excitement. Just before I made it to the hole, an arm shot out and stopped me, hugging me tightly against a familiar chest. "No, Kaede. Let the boys handle it."

"Uncle Tatsuo! Let me go, please." Panic seeped into my voice as I struggled against him.

"He is your protector. You are not his."

"Does that really go to the dungeon?"

"To the stairwell leading to the dungeon. What kind of jail would it be if it were on the ground floor?"

"Did she escape?"

"I do not know. I arrived just in time to stop you from doing something monumentally stupid."

"Why now? Where were you the other three-point-five million times?" I growled in frustration, unable to take my eyes from the smoking darkness.

We stood there, unable to move, until Remy came striding through the hole, blazer covering his nose and mouth. The rest of him was covered in soot. He immediately headed for Tatsuo and me. When Roki's head appeared behind him, I started breathing again, and Uncle Tatsuo let me go.

Luckily, Roki had caught up to Remy. Tackling them simultaneously made things a little easier. "Don't you do that again!" I spoke to both of them, meaning it.

"She's gone," Remy whispered.

They were both holding me. My tackle hadn't gone exactly as planned, and I was actually clinging to both of them at the same time. Slowly, I slid to the ground and stood before them. "I know she was a bitch, but I'm sorry for your loss, Rem."

He blinked in confusion and shook his head. "No. She's *gone*. Escaped. Not here."

"Oh! Thank, *Kami*. Wait. Scratch that. Whut?"

He nodded, the worried look on his face out-worrying mine exponentially.

"Did I hear you correctly?" Uncle Tatsuo's voice behind me caused me to jump a little and spin.

"Don't *do* that!" I swatted him in the chest. He lifted an eyebrow at me.

"Yes, Headmaster. She escaped."

Tatsuo sighed and rubbed the bridge of his nose. "You and your brother sweep the school grounds. Have the disciplinary committee aid you. I doubt she remained on campus, but one never knows. In the meantime, locate Stephanie. Your sister could not have escaped without aid." He paused a moment to stare at me. "Where is your Geri?"

"Lewis?"

"Not Gerry. Geri. Where is she?"

"I don't know? We don't really hang out. I don't think she likes me very much."

"She has little choice, and you are well aware of that fact. Close your eyes and find her."

"Okely dokely." I closed my eyes as he asked and thought about Meg, Geri's real name. The one Fenrir had taken from her when he made her mine. "She's in her room, reading." I opened my eyes and looked back at my draconic uncle.

"I did not think she had part in this, but it is better to be sure." He looked at Remy over my shoulder. "Find Stephanie."

"Yes, Headmaster," he answered and took off.

Tatsuo looked at Hiroki, and something wordlessly passed between them before he turned around and walked away without so much as a goodbye.

"What was that about?" I asked Hiroki.

"I am to keep you safe."

"Duh," I said and leaned back against him, trusting he would be there. He didn't disappoint me, but his smell did. "Uh, keep me safe after a shower. You smell like a briquette."

∞ ∞ ∞

"Knock, knock," I said as I entered David's room in the infirmary, instantly regretting it. He was asleep in the metal framed bed that seemed a little too small for him. I paused in the doorway, smiling at him. A stray ray of sunshine was filtering through the curtains, illuminating his face.

He blinked as he woke, saw me, and smiled.

"Hey, Kaede."

"Hey, yourself. How are you feeling?"

"Tired, but fine."

Walking into the room, I slipped into the chair beside the bed, leaving Geri in the doorway. Before Roki would go take a shower, he made me call her to my side, telling me in no uncertain terms that the odds of me being alone at any point until Sabine was found were absolute zero. He even made sure Geri had a blade before he grabbed his toiletries and headed to get cleaned up, promising to meet us at the infirmary.

"When do you get out of here?"

"How are you doing? I heard about Sabine." He frowned, ignoring my question.

"I'm fine. I doubt she escaped from the dungeon to come after me. She's probably in Sri Lanka by now."

"Sri Lanka?"

"Yeah. It's a country."

"I know what it is and where it is, why did you pick there?"

"I just like saying it. Say it with me. Shreeeeee Lanka. Sounds like a fun place."

David blinked, not knowing if I was joking or not.

Geri just snickered from the door.

The nurse came into the small room and immediately swept up to David, grabbing his wrist and feeling his pulse while looking at her watch. "Is this the Kaede I've been hearing so much about?"

"It is," David answered with a smile.

I frowned. "I is."

Staring at the gorgeous blonde of indeterminate age and smallish outfit, I felt the hair on the back of my neck bristle in outrage. His nurse was supposed to be a mountain troll or something as equally hideous. Not some svelte Swedish Danish (the pastry kind, not the people) with Alps for a chest. "Pleased to finally meet you, I am Lornca." She let go of David's wrist and held out her hand.

Reluctantly, I took it and forced a smile on my face as we shook. "I'm Kaede. David's *girlfriend*."

"Yes. I know. He talks about you all the time. Even in his sleep. It is quite cute. You have a beautiful name."

"Thank you. You watch him while he sleeps?"

"It is my job, yes." She gave me a funny look that I didn't find funny at all.

"How much longer?"

"Pardon?"

"How much longer 'til he can…go back to class? Sleep in his room. Leave the infirmary."

A frown settled on her overly pouty lips. "I am unsure. He is not getting his strength back as quickly as I had hoped."

I turned my attention back to David. He shrugged and struggled to sit up a little. Her hand pressed him back down against the bed, and she shot him an angry look. "Rest. Have a visit with your girlfriend and get some sleep." She looked up at me. "Stay with him, but not too long, okay? He needs his strength. Come see me when you are done."

"Thank you, Lornca," I said meekly, feeling horrible that David's condition was not improving.

She nodded and left us alone.

"Gosh. She's pretty." I raised an eyebrow at David once she was gone.

"If you're into elves."

"Elves?"

"Yep. She's from Alfheim."

"Oh, goody. She hasn't given you a sponge bath, has she?" I couldn't help it. It was the first question that popped into my head the moment I saw her, and it had been fighting to claw its way out of my mouth.

"What?"

"Sponge. Bath. You smell awfully clean."

"Well…yes, but it was just her cleaning me up. Not my proudest moment."

"So, hot, tall, and sexy rubs a soapy little sponge all over you, and you weren't standing proud and tall?"

"Uh…if you mean what I think you mean, then no."

"No movement?"

"Not even a twitch."

"Okay. You live. No twitchies." I poked him in the offending member.

"Well if *you're* gonna do that, no promises."

"I'm going to go jump off something really tall," Geri said from the doorway with an exasperated sigh. Then she turned around and faced outside the room, leaning against the jamb.

I giggled and poked him again.

"Kaede, stop!"

Smiling at him, I stood up, and then gave him a concerned look. "Get better. Quickly. I *miss* you." I leaned in and gave him a chaste kiss, not wanting to walk away leaving him all turned on and shit with a hot nurse giving him sponge baths.

"I'm trying."

"Do. There is no try or do nots. Get better, David. I mean it."

"Yes, ma'am." He winked at me.
"I love you."
"Love you, too. My little vixen."

Chapter 3

The spoon shook slightly as Professor Welheim slowly lifted it to her gnarled face portal. I had to forcibly drive the image of someone spoon feeding an anus from my brain as I watched her slurp my cream of asparagus soup and make appreciative clucking noises with her tentacle-like tongue. No, she wasn't a sea hag, she was just that ugly. Picture that aunt who only shows up on holidays, loves to hug you, and smells like a cross between mothballs and hippo balls.

She blinked in surprise.

My heart stopped. I'd finally done it and accidentally poisoned my teacher. It wasn't my fault Hiroki had been called to the office, and I'd warned her that I shouldn't be allowed to cook without supervision, but she'd insisted. Now she was going to pay for her mistake with her life.

"Miss Tanaka?"

"Yes, Professor?"

"That is delicious. Well done."

Oh, thank fuck. While her demise would have meant a more relaxed classroom atmosphere, I didn't relish in the thought of being Sabine's cellmate in the Aesir Academy dungeon. Once they caught her again. "Thank you, Professor."

She tossed the tasting spoon into the sink at the end of the station I shared with Roki and moved on to the next pair of fearful students. As soon as her back was turned, I opened the cabinet and took a long swig of mead from the plastic bottle I had filled during the cooking competition.

Not being party to first-degree murder deserved a reward. Even mead.

While the sweet honey wine was a nice respite from the monotony of *sake*, I found myself missing the acidic burn of the only alcohol I'd been able to drink since birth. Not that I came out of the womb sucking down *sake*, but my inari fox half could create it as soon as we came into our power. A gift from the *Inari-kami* for our service. Since Fenrir had stolen me away from him, I'd ended up a honey sucker.

Do you not like my gift? I can take it away…

The image of suffering through Home Economics without any type of booze scared the ever-loving shit out of me. *No! I am grateful. Thank you!*

His mental chuckle faded just as the door to the classroom opened, and a very fearful looking Hiroki walked in. I took one last swig of mead and stuffed the bottle back into the cabinet, not caring for the worried look he was giving me as he walked over.

"What's wrong?" I didn't even give him a chance to sit down before blurting out the question. I could feel the fear coming off him in waves. Big waves. Fear tsunamis.

He just shook his head and sat down on the gray, metal stool beside me. "It is nothing, Kaede-*sama.*"

"Nothing doesn't make you look like somebody just ran over your kitten. Spill your guts. What happened?"

"Your father is here."

The earth stopped spinning and rotating around the sun. The drop of sweat on Roki's forehead that had been slowly slithering down to the bridge of his nose halted its descent. Professor Welheim's inane chatter stopped mid-sentence at the precise moment my heart stopped beating. "What?"

"Your father. He is here. In Headmaster Tatsuo's office."

"Oh." Time began slowly ticking forward again. My heart restarted with a resounding *thwump*. I knew he was going to show up sooner or later. I was just hoping for later. Much later. Maybe for graduation. Then anger replaced my fear. "Wait a damn minute… He called you to Tatsuo's office and not me?"

Roki blinked, and then slowly nodded. "*Hai.*"

"What did he want?"

"He wished for clarification as to some of the events that had…occurred."

"And he couldn't ask me?"

"I do not know, Kaede-*sama.*" He stared off, lost in thought.

I took another swig of honey-flavored joy juice. *Fuck it. I'm getting nuked, and then napalming the school.*

"Miss Tanaka. I do believe I told you that beverages are not permitted in class…"

"Sorry, Professor Velkkkheim." I made her name extra juicy and chugged the rest of the contents of the bottle.

∞ ∞ ∞

"You put one foot in front of the other," I sang as I ran around the track, concentrating on not tripping or puking. Roki ran next to me, probably to catch me if I fell. He was trying to be unobtrusive but failing miserably. Every time I staggered, he frantically reached out to catch me. It was kind of cute, and I started to make a game of it. Even exclaiming, "Woah," with every other step and wobbling a little.

"Your father could appear at any moment to check on you, and you choose to become slovenly drunk?"

"I didn't choose to drink, Roki. The drink chose me."

"It chose poorly."

"Are you saying I'm a shitty drunk?"

"No. I am saying you have abysmal timing. Wait. Yes, you are a shitty drunk."

I chuckled and started singing again, the presence of my father at the school somewhat blurred by inebriation. As was my name. The only clear thought in my brain was smiling and waving at David every time I passed by him.

He'd *finally* been released from the infirmary. Unfortunately for me, he'd also been relegated to the ranks of sitting on the sidelines and watching the kids in full health run around the track until they were no longer at full health. I was kind of jelly. I wanted to sit with him. We could make fun of Hiroki together. Plus, it was too damn cold to be running outside. We were going to catch something that ended in *itis* or *monia*.

I must have been grinning and waving a little too hard. I stumbled and fell, Hiroki's hands grabbing me just before I faceplanted into the concrete track. "Thanks, Roki."

"Be *careful*, Kaede-*sama*."

"Careful, shmareful. The track rippled."

"I shall give it a stern talking to. Go sit with your David. I shall let the coach know you are not feeling well."

"Thanks, Roki. You're the most bestest." I glanced over at Coach Cobb and made sure he wasn't looking before I planted a quick kiss on Hiroki's lips. He blushed slightly as I turned and walked very slowly and steadily over to David. "Hey, handsome."

"Hi, Grace."

"Grace?"

He motioned to the track and smacked his palm with the other. "Graceful."

"Oh. You saw that."

"Couldn't take my eyes off of you."

Heat crept up my face and to other places as I sat down on the cold metal bleachers and tried to ignore the chill creeping its way into my buttocks.

"Cold?"

"Could you tell from the shivers, or me shifting from cheek to cheek?"

"Bit of both. Don't worry, your butt will warm the metal."

"Or freeze solid."

"That, too."

"Think the coach would notice if we slipped away to someplace warmer?"

"Probably."

I sighed until David leaned a little closer and put his arm around me, instantly defrosting me with his werewolf thermonuclear body temperature. I squealed and buried my face in his shoulder, fighting the temptation to crawl into his lap and live there for all eternity. Or at least until summer rolled around.

"Better?"

"Mmph mmph." It was hard to speak with my face buried in his sweatshirt.

I wrapped my arms around his stomach and turned my head, watching the poor unfortunate souls running around the track. Roki smiled as he passed, and I gave him a little wave.

"He seems much happier."

"Roki?"

"Yeah."

"Well, I'm sure it has a lot to do with getting laid."

David's bark of laughter jarred my little head. "I think it has to do with a little more than that."

"Oh? Do tell, great sage of the Moon Clan."

"I think it has more to do with who was doing the laying."

"*Moi?*"

"Of course. That man has been in love with you forever and a day. He's probably riding cloud nine right now."

I sat up a little straighter, putting my lips near David's ear. "Maybe it was having your cock in his mouth. I know that made *me* happy."

The heat from his face doubled in intensity. "I uh… Um. Yeah. Wow."

"Did you forget about that?" I chuckled softly in his ear.

"No."

"I sure didn't." I licked his ear for emphasis and laughed when he coughed.

I let go of him, letting my arm drop and accidentally brushing against his semi-erection. Looking at him in shock, I slowly cocked an eyebrow.

"What?"

"Somebody's got some happy memories floating through his widdle noggin..." I poked him in the chest.

He shifted in his seat. "Totally unrelated. You're very warm."

"So was Roki's mouth. Wasn't it?"

He slumped in his seat, slightly pouting. "Yes."

"You liked it, didn't you?" I grinned at him.

"Yes."

"Wanna do it again?"

He looked up and blinked. "Uh..."

The way he was struggling with it was beyond adorable. "You're worried people will think you're gay?"

His eyes narrowed, and he shook his head. "No. Not at all."

"Good, cuz I would have had to clobber you with a rubber dick."

"You'd like that too much."

I grinned at him. "Bet your ass."

"That is the last place a rubber dick is going..."

I couldn't help completely losing it and laughing until the tears streamed down my face. "Come on... I'll call you Peggy."

"Peggy?"

"Pegging?"

"Do I even want to know what that is? Or how you know about it?"

"What? It's when a girl wears a strap on."

"Strap on what?"

"You can't be that naïve. Can you?' It was my turn to blink in surprise. "Don't you ever watch porn?"

"Yes? Of girls masturbating. Sometimes I watch lesbian porn."

"All guys do. Didn't you ever browse any of the other categories?"

He blushed.

Bingo. I didn't want to know what David's kinks were. I *needed* to know.

"You can tell me," I coaxed him gently.

"Sometimes. I like to uh watch…"

"What? Spit roasts? Threesomes?"

"What's a spit roast? I know what a threesome is. I've watched that."

"I'll show you later. What is it you're into? Glory holes? Squirting? Exhibitionism? Voyeurism? Creampies? DP? BDSM? CFNM? Sybian? Golden showers? What? Oh, please don't say scat. I can't handle that. That's just nasty."

I was getting further and further away from the mark. I could tell by the deepening confusion on his face. "Was that even English?"

"Kinda. Tell you what… *You* tell me. What is it you like, David?"

He looked around to make sure nobody was close enough to listen. *After* I blurted out a good portion of the Porn Hub library, he worried. Leaning in and putting his lips next to my ear, he finally whispered. "Upskirts."

I pulled away and stared at him to see if he was joking. He wasn't. I could see the excitement on his face. He was excited just by saying the word. "Upskirt what?"

The excitement was replaced by confusion. "That's it."

"You like looking up women's skirts? That's the big secret?"

He nodded.

"Oh, my sweet summer child. I love you."

"You think I'm gross?"

"What? Why?"

"Because I like seeing panties?"

And there it was. David's kryptonite. With that knowledge, I would conquer the earth. "Hate to break it to you, sweetie. Every guy does."

"They do?"

"Yerp."

He let out a breath I hadn't realized he'd been holding. "Oh, thank Fen–"

I slapped my hand over his mouth and shook my head. "Nerp. Nerp. Nerp. Do not say his name."

He nodded, and I pulled my hand away from his mouth. "Sorry."

"It's okay. I know it's a force of habit."

"So, it doesn't bother you that I like upskirt shots?"

"Hell, no. Sorry my panties are boring."

His blush spoke volumes.

"What?"

"Plain white cotton… Yeah. I like them."

The village had KFC. *Maybe*, they would have a Victoria's Secret. If he liked plain white cotton, white lace would blow his mind. Or other things. "You just opened up a whole can of worms, you know that, right?"

"Huh?"

"If I had known, I would have flashed you a whole lot more. I just wish we had more classes together. Either way, this is gonna be *fun*."

"You're going to flash me?"

"Whenever and wherever I can. Don't want you looking up other girls' skirts."

"I would never…"

"Bullshit. Hell, I do." I grinned. "Tell you what. If we're together, and I see somebody accidentally flashing, I'll point it out to you. We can look together." I winked, and he groaned, apparently liking the idea. I purposely ran my hand over his previously semi-erection. There was nothing semi about it. Except maybe the load he was hauling. I chuckled evilly. "Oh, you *really* like that," I said and left my hand in his lap, lightly touching him through his sweatpants.

"Kaede," he hissed my name. "There's people."

"Don't look at me. I'm not touching *their* junk. Perv."

"No! I mean mine. We're going to get busted."

"There's no way in hell. Look at them. They're running little miserable circles around the track. Plus, this is kind of hot." I took him between my fingers and slowly slid my hand up and down, letting the softness of his sweatpants glide over him. He shuddered next to me, obviously enjoying the sensation.

"Yes, but the wet spot on the front of my pants is going to be very noticeable."

"Guess you'll just have to run to the locker room after class. Gosh, I hope nobody sees." I grinned at him.

"Kaede!"

"David!" I said, mocking his exasperation and taking delight at his fluttering eyes.

If he had made *any* motion to stop me, I would have in a heartbeat. Hell, if he even *told* me to stop, I would have. Saying that there were people around wasn't clear enough.

"Do you want me to stop?" Even though I knew the answer, I asked anyway.

"No," he answered meekly.

My subtle ministrations became a little more forceful, only slowing when the possibility of discovery became *too* much. David's breathing took on a frantic pace I knew only too well. He was about to come. I grinned and tried to double my efforts without being noticed.

Roki was rounding the bend again, I gave him a wicked grin and waved with my free hand. He smiled for an instant, but then his eyes focused slightly above me and a horrified look crossed his face. I turned, and from the look on his face, I half expected Uncle Tatsuo to be in his draconic form, setting the school ablaze with his fiery breath.

"Greetings, Daughter," My father's voice stopped my hand and my heart in their tracks.

Chapter 4

Setting the tray down on the worn wooden table for two, I meekly sat down and folded my hands together in my lap as I waited for my father to join me. Hiroki, he called to the office. Me, he stalked during gym class and insisted that I have a private lunch with him before the dining hall filled with students. I hadn't been envious of Hiroki, but staring at my nearly empty plate of food, getting called to the headmaster's office seemed like the better of the two options. At least then, I would have been able to grub.

"Not like I'm hungry, anyway," I said to no one in particular.

Yes, you are. You always are. Fenrir's voice chuckled softly in my head.

Oh, no. No, you don't. Go lie down somewhere. I can't deal with you and *my father at the same time. I can barely deal with him.*

You would rather rise the ire of a god than your father?

Fuck yes.

I like him. I shall be…unobtrusive. His laughter was anything but.

When I opened my eyes, eyes I hadn't even realized I'd closed while talking to Fenrir, my father was sitting at the table across from me, hands folded under his chin, watching me intently. I might have screamed a little bit.

"You were conversing with him."

I nodded, not trusting my voice.

Sighing, he sat forward and moved one of the cups of tea from his tray to mine. "Fear not, Daughter. We shall mend the damage that has been done." He unrolled the napkin and stared in horror at the fork that tumbled out, skidding to a stop atop the thick plastic tray.

"What is the matter?"

"They do not have chopsticks?"

"No. Only about five percent of the school population is Asian."

"I figured with Tatsuo as the headmaster, all of you would be using chopsticks by now. No matter, I do know how to use a fork."

I sighed and unrolled mine, grabbing it and jabbing it through a clump of lettuce from my salad. Salads were for bunnies. Even ranch dressing didn't help mask the taste of healthy.

"Why do you eat it if you despise it?"

"Because it's good for me."

"Judging by the face you are making, you would not be partaking if I were not here."

"Sure, I would. Just like Roki. I live, breathe, and shit salads."

"Language, Daughter."

"Sorry, Father." I sighed and slinked down a little in my seat.

"Sit up."

"Yes, Father."

Why are you eating that which you do not like? Feast upon the flesh of lesser creatures!

Men?

That shut him up.

"What does he say?"

How my father knew I was talking to Fenrir again was a complete mystery. But, then again, he was a full Inari Fox. He could probably feel it. "That I should eat my vegetables."

"I am sure," my father answered drolly, rolling his eyes. Then he stared at me thoughtfully for a moment. With yet another sigh, he reached over and touched the side of my teacup with one finger, and the side of his with

42

one from his other hand. The fragrant smell of tea around us dissipated, turning into something cleaner and more sterile smelling. *Sake.*

I cocked an eyebrow at my father. He was not one to *ever* condone my drinking, let alone contribute. "Thank you?"

"You have been having a rough time of it lately. I figured you could use a little reward."

Smiling in gratitude, I lifted the cup and inhaled deeply. I had the ability to make sake, but I had to mix rice with water. My father could transmute any liquid into *sake.* It was probably a good thing I hadn't been born with that particular power. As soon as the warm wetness touched my tongue, I rolled it around and waited for the familiar tingle that never came. It still burned, but with sweetness.

Really? You couldn't let him have this one moment? You had to turn his sake *into mead?*

That is a drink unfit to clean an empty barrel of mead.

My father raised his cup in gesture and took a sip. His eyes widened and he spit the drink to the floor beside him, sputtering and wiping his mouth with a napkin. "What is this?"

I sighed. *This isn't going to end well.* "It is mead, Father."

"You did this?"

I shook my head. "It's been over a month since I've had *sake.* I was looking forward to that."

"It was him," he said and stood, staring down at me and our two cups.

"Yes, Father."

"Come with me," he said sternly, turning and heading toward the exit without so much as looking back to make sure I was following him.

I gulped down my cup and then his as I passed. By the time we had left the dining hall, I had caught up to him. "Where are we going?"

He held up his hand in answer, his anger causing his foxfire to flare behind him into three swirling spheres.

Another trick I had never mastered. Useful in battle, dangerous when drunk. Maybe it was a good thing I sucked at being a celestial messenger. Fenrir would probably be picking his teeth with Odin's bones if I didn't.

You are an excellent herald. Quite amusing.

Gee, thanks.

Do not mention it.

Even the god who had been asleep for thousands of years made fun of me.

My father stopped, fire flaring in his eyes as he rounded on me. "You will stop talking to him this instant!"

I opened my mouth to say, "Yes father." I swear I did. Upon all that is holy. "She is mine," came out a few dozen octaves lower than I could ever have pulled off. There was even a hint of *snarl* in my voice. Either I had the world's nastiest chest cold and developed a love for talking about myself in the third person, or Fenrir was driving the Kaedemobile.

The fiery blue orbs above my father flared in the wake of his anger. "Relinquish your hold on my daughter, now!"

"And let her go back to your faded master? I do not think so."

My father blinked at me. Fenrir had been speaking through me again, but this time, using my own voice. The effect was kind of creepy.

"That wasn't me!" I held up my hands to protest my innocence.

"Yes, it was," Fenrir said with my mouth and his voice.

Stop getting me into trouble! I don't need your damn help. I get in trouble just fine on my own!

"Kaede?"

One of the twins had rounded the corner and was staring at me and my father. He looked at me in tense confusion, muscles rippling beneath his jacket, uncertain if he should protect me from the obviously Japanese man standing in front of me with fire swirling around him. A man who didn't look much older than me, but who had the grace and wisdom of kings tucked around him like a fine-tailored suit. "Hey, Rome…"

"Remy."

"That's what I said. This is my father…"

Remy relaxed and gave my father a small bow. "Hello, Mr. Tanaka."

"And you are?" My father turned from me, and his fire dwindled.

"Remy Lateran. I have the privilege of being your daughter's…" He trailed off because I was doing jumping jacks behind my father and shaking my head, mouthing the word no. "Classmate," he finished with a smile.

Thank fuck.

"Pleasure to meet you. Come, Kaede. We have much to discuss," my father answered, not taking his eyes off Remy until he walked past him.

I stood up on my tiptoes and kissed him gently on the lips as I passed, not daring to take *my* eyes off my father. "I'll uh…see you later Remy. Thanks for taking notes for me." I gave him a small smile and hurried to catch up with my father's long strides.

It took us nearly ten minutes to get to the headmaster's office, and my father didn't utter a single word during the entire trek. Without so much as a knock, he opened the door and ushered me into the room with a very surprised looking Tatsuo sitting behind his desk.

"What did you do?"

Yep. He's family. "Nothing, this time."

"It is not her. It is that damnable creature in her head," my father answered angrily, slamming the door shut. "We need to sever the connection between them. Their occasional conversation has turned into relentless banter."

Tatsuo looked to me for confirmation. I wanted to lie. Hell, I wanted to hide. But I didn't. "He seems kind of lonely."

"Why did you say nothing?"

"Hey, Unk. That god that used to sometimes talk to me once in a while? Yeah. He won't shut up."

You would miss me, little one…

And then it happened. There was a ghostly caress that slid across my skin, in a place he had *no* business touching. I gasped and shivered, and not in a good way. *Do not do that! Ever. Especially in front of my father.*

I know not of what you speak. His chuckle told me he was full of shit.

"Kaede?" Uncle Tatsuo had stood without my noticing. His fingers were pressed against the surface of his desk as he stared at me concernedly.

"Yes?"

"What just happened?"

"Nothing."

His eyes narrowed, but he let it go when I glanced nervously at my father. Thankfully, he was looking at his draconic friend for guidance. There were just some things that didn't need to be discussed in front of one's father. Tatsuo turned to my father. "You were right. It would seem he has become quite enamored with your daughter. As to breaking the bond, I do not know how, or if, it can be done. We should, however, not discuss it in front of his tie to the mortal realm." He turned to me. "You are dismissed. Your father and I will continue this conversation."

He gave me the out I so desperately wanted. Bless his lizard face. "Yes, Headmaster," I said respectfully and turned to my father. "Father."

I didn't run to the door, but I power-walked in desperation. There was a cafeteria with my name on it. Maybe if I started referring to it as Kaede Hall, it would catch on, and they would have to put up a plaque or something.

They can talk all they wish. Our bond is stronger than the chains that bind me, never to be severed.

That doesn't give you permission to touch me in my no-no square, I snarled with a bit of anger. *Keep your finger of god out of my tornado alley.*

You do not wish to be wooed by a god? His chuckle caressed me lightly, sending shivers up my arms and down my back.

Don't woo my hooha. This is not three-thousand years ago. I'll have your ass tossed in jail for assault, and then you can explain to your cellmate how you inappropriately touched a schoolgirl.

I do not understand your words, but I can see the scenario painted in your mind. Do you think a mortal jail is a threat? Or a hairy man with a penchant for same sex trysts?

I'd been walking down the hall, lost in conversation. Everything had been going great until I slammed into a large, masculine, and familiar chest.

"Kaede!" Remy stopped me from flying back and landing ass first onto the marble floor. "Are you okay? I called your name three times."

"Yeah. Just lost in thought. Sorry." I got up on my tiptoes and kissed him squarely on the lips. He tensed, and I knew it was Rome. "Sorry for running into you, Rome." I played it off like I knew who from who and took a step back.

"You knew it was me?"

"Yes? Why?"

He gently touched his lips with two fingers and gave me a happy little smile, until he realized what he was doing, and his face contorted into resting bitch face. I wished he wouldn't do that. He was a thousand times handsomer when he smiled. "Are you hungry?"

"Are you Italian?"

The faintest hint of that dazzling smile made its way back into the corner of his mouth. "Care to eat with me?"

"Thought you'd never ask." Grabbing his arm in mine, I started pulling him toward Kaede Hall and its endless buffet.

"Kaede," Rome started but trailed off as we were walking.

"What?"

"Why did you kiss me?"

"Because I wanted to."

"And you knew it was me?"

"Of course."

He got quiet after that, but stopped me just as we were about to enter the overly crowded dining hall. "Then why did you kiss me?"

"Because I wanted to," I reiterated slowly.

"Why? Why did you want to kiss me? That is what I am asking."

"Oh. I don't know. I like you."

"You do? This isn't some game you're playing?"

"Of course not."

Liar.

Shut your face. I do like him. I just wish he was a little less grumpy.

"Because, I'm going to be honest. When you're not driving me insane, I like you, too. But I'm tired of you only showering me with affection when you mistake me for my brother. That bothers me."

Guilt warred with the hunger inside me. "Rome... I like you. A lot. How could I not? You're a bit more surly than I like, and we definitely got off on the wrong four feet, but when you're not being a grump ass, you're sweet, caring, protective, and hot as all fuck. If you like me, ask me to be your girlfriend. Quit reading so much into everything."

"I cannot help it. The alpha of the pack has to see everything from every possible angle."

"Pretty sure that is the acceptable response for danger, not dating."

"You don't think you're dangerous?" He let out a short bark of laughter and smirked at me.

"Little old me? Ain't got a dangerous bone in my body." I looked down below his belt. "Yet."

He blushed furiously red. My work was done.

"Food?"

He rolled his eyes. "You and your insatiable appetites."

"You ain't seen nothing yet."

"That's what I'm afraid of."

We filled our plates and glasses. Surprisingly, Rome carried both of our trays to the large circular table in the corner. He set them down and then took both drinks from my hands, placing them neatly beside the heaping plates of food before pulling out my chair. "My lady."

"Such a gentlewolf."

"Shhh," he said softly, winking to soften his rebuke. "Not everyone in this school is your friend."

"Me? Everybody loves me."

He patted me on my head as I sat down. "Four out of a thousand is a small percentage."

"Five. Uncle Tatsuo adores me."

"Six. Your father is here from what I heard."

"As I said. Five. But it's the five that matter most." I grinned at him and shoved some food in my mouth that wasn't green and leafy. Meaty and cheesy was so much better, and I sighed in relief.

I had just taken a bite of my second chicken leg when Remy sat his tray on the other side of me, David and Roki right after him. I sighed as a feeling of happy settled over me that had nothing to do with stuffing food down my happy little gullet. *Rarely*, did the five of us get to eat together, and it was almost overwhelming as I looked around the table.

"What is it, Kaede-*sama*?" Leave it to Roki to pick up on my mood.

Blushing, I shook my head at him. "Just happy."

"And you are only halfway done with your food." He smiled at his own joke.

"Yes, but the night still young." I did what I did best. I ate.

The food was good, the conversation was great, and the company was the best. I had just set my fork down on the edge of my plate, when I felt the first chill of fear race down my spine. There was no explanation for it, just the chill of murderous intent from behind me. Then the look of

49

utter shock and fear as Roki stared over my shoulder. I managed to turn around just in time to see the look of hatred on Sabine's cloaked form as she slipped out of her all too familiar interdimensional pocket and drove the glowing blue dagger into my chest.

Falling backward against the table, I slid from the chair and onto the floor just as the icy grip of death clutched my heart and squeezed. Everything inside me turned to ice as the room faded to black. Rome and Remy, Hiroki and David's voices breaking my heart as they screamed my name in despair. Unfortunately, the last sound I heard was Sabine's grating cackle.

At least I got to finish my dinner.

Chapter 5

There was three feet of snow on the ground, but I didn't feel the slightest bit of chill as I crossed the worn pathway leading to the largest set of wooden doors I'd ever seen in my entire short life. They had to have been over twenty feet high. Nobody short of a giant was going to be breaking into the gleaming silver castle anytime soon. Especially me. Unfortunately, I couldn't stop my feet from propelling me toward the doors. No matter how hard I tried, I couldn't stop walking.

When I drew close enough, they opened by themselves.

They didn't make a noise, either. "That's kind of creepy."

My voice was the only sound. No birds, animals, or people disturbed the silence surrounding me. Even my voice sounded muffled in my ears. I would have given my last jar of *sake* for the familiar hum of traffic or the sound of the students of Aesir Academy.

As soon as they crossed the threshold, my feet stopped propelling me forward like a zombie. The temperature inside was the same as outside, and I felt neither relief nor discomfort from the protection from the elements.

"Hello? Pardon the intrusion," I called out from years of habit.

"Hello, child." The feminine voice came from everywhere and nowhere. I could feel it in the walls and in my bones.

"Uh, hi?"

"Do you know where you are?"

"Not a friggin' clue."

"Do you know who I am? Do your people still sing songs of me and my home? Sessrumnir?"

"Maaaybe. Don't have it on my playlist though… What's a Sessru…mawhatcher?"

Her chuckle sent a tingling sensation through my ears and down my spine. I spun and looked up at the stone staircase that had been hidden against the back wall, leading up to the floors above. She smiled as she descended. My voice caught in my throat at her beauty.

She wasn't young as far as gods went. Or at least she didn't look so to my highly trained eyes, but neither did she appear old. Regal would have been the perfect word to describe her. She wore a white gossamer dress over white doe-skin boots. A silver circlet made sure no stray strands of red hair swept from her tight braid and into her piercing blue eyes.

"Um, who are you?"

She paused a moment on the stairs and gave me a sad smile. "One of the many gods of this land. You may call me Freya."

The blood in my veins froze. The chill that I hadn't felt outside crept into my bones. I knew her all right. Uncle Tatsuo had versed me in almost every god of every religion, but he had been particularly meticulous with the Norse pantheon. I didn't understand why until I got my ass shipped off to Iceland and enrolled at Aesir Academy, named after one of the two clans of gods. Freya was Vanir, but had been given to the Aesir as part of a peace treaty. She was even married to Odin at one time.

My knees started shaking uncontrollably, and I probably would have dropped to the floor of her keep had my feet not still been rooted firmly to the floor.

"Uh, hi. I'm–"

"Kaede," she answered for me.

"Oh, right. Goddess. Derp."

"Do you know why you are here?"

I knew. Saying it out loud was a completely different animal, though. "Fenrir."

She had the Nordic word for *cajones* to actually laugh. I thought she was teasing me, but she shook her head and continued down the remainder of the stairs. Her hand reached out and gripped my shoulder gently as she ushered me through one of the many adjoining archways and into a small, but comfortable looking room with two opposing couches with a wooden table nestled between them. "No. Fenrir is the reason I am going to send you back."

She bade me sit on one couch and unceremoniously sat across from me, closing her beautiful eyes for a moment and listening.

"Send me back to school?"

Her eyes opened, and a look of pity flashed through them. "Yes. Would you care for something to drink?"

"When wouldn't I?"

"Pardon?"

"Yes, please, your grace."

"Freya will suffice," she answered with a smile, just as a slender woman in a green dress walked into the room carrying a tray with a pitcher and two glasses.

"My lady," she said and put the tray on the table, pouring a goblet full of honey colored liquid and offering it to the goddess.

"Mead?"

"Something better…" She winked and waited for the servant to pour me a glass. When she did, I gasped. Her pupils were slit like a cat's and were three different colors, each winding around the other, and her ears were pointed. I was staring at an honest to goodness elf. Lornca was an elf, too, but appeared human with pointed ears. The one standing in front of me had inhuman eyes, long tapered ears, and her skin was almost green. She was beautiful.

I lifted my left hand, the one not holding the goblet of whatever she had poured for me and spread my fingers between my middle and ring finger. "Live long, preposterously."

"Pardon?"

"Nothing. Thank you for the wine."

She bowed and left Freya and I sitting there, the goddess staring at me, and me staring at the floor trying not to feel like an insignificant bug. "So, why am I here?"

"Do you remember getting here?"

"Yeah. It was a long friggin' walk, ten miles through the snow barefoot, uphill both ways."

"And what were you doing before that?"

"Eating and getting *stabbed!*" My hand started shaking, and I almost dropped the goblet. Clutching it in both hands, I managed to get it to my lips and take giant gulp.

I swallowed fucking fire.

Literal flames licked my gullet as I tried to swallow, gave up, and let the liquid dribble out of my mouth onto my chest. The only thing I could do was lick my sleeves. So, I did.

"Are you all right?"

"Ntho. That burnthed."

"You are supposed to sip it, not inhale." She was laughing at me. In fact, when she wiped the corners of her eyes, little drops of amber fell to the polished floor.

"Wait. How am I here? Am I dead? Why does liquor burn a dead person? Should I even be able to drink? Where exactly is here?"

"Slow down."

"Sorry. Not every day you die."

"Not unless you are cursed."

"Am I?"

"No. I think you might actually lead a semi-charmed life, child. You died in battle. The odds were half that you would end up here."

"And the other half?"

"In care of Odin."

"And that would be bad?"

"If you wished to spend the rest of your existence here, no. But the odds of you ever seeing Midgard again would be nil."

"Oh. So…you're going to send me back?"

She nodded. "Once the mortals around you get over the shock of your untimely demise and try to heal you. I shall."

I set the goblet down on the table and stood up, slapping my knees as I did. "Sweet!"

"Sit."

I sat.

"You're not even going to ask why I'm going to send you back?"

"I'm sure you have your reasons."

"Or at what cost to you?"

"Do you like rice? My parents have a *ton* of it. Like literally tons. I can hook you up."

"I need you to focus."

"I don't think I can. I mean, you're not the first person, I mean goddess, to ask me that. Okay, you might be the first goddess, but literally hundreds of people, teachers, et cetera, have tried to get me to focus. I mean, there are prescription medications that would probably help if I wasn't a kitsune-Inari half-breed. I mean, I tried some Adderall at a club one time, but Special K seemed to work a little better, but that was more sleepy than focusy–"

She snapped her fingers, and my voice left me. I tried talking but only a bunch of wheezing sounds came out. "There. That's better."

I blinked at her in Morse code.

"As I was saying, I *will* send you back once they heal that fragile mortal coil of yours. I am keeping your heart beating slowly. Hopefully, you do not lose too much of your life blood before they can magic you back to health. Make no mistake, if it were not for my power, you would truly be dead, and there would be no going back. Consider it payment for the services you are going to render."

I blinked at her in confusion.

"You are going to kill Fenrir."

I blinked at her in shock. *Then* I looked around the room worriedly. If he even had an inkling…

"Do not worry. He cannot find you here. This memory, and our plans to rid the nine realms of any danger he poses, will be locked behind an unbreakable seal in that little brain of yours."

I blinked in consternation.

She stood up and walked around the table, taking another sip of her god-wine before setting the goblet down. I cringed away from her. She scared me a thousand times more than Fenrir ever had.

Deftly dodging the goblet with her ass, she sat down on the table in front of me and leaned closer, her nose nearly touching mine. "Are you afraid?"

I nodded.

"Good. That is as it should be. Fenrir is formidable. I do not envy the position he has put you in."

I opened my mouth to speak, gazing at her imploringly. With a snap of her fingers, my voice came back to me. "Help me."

"I am helping you."

"Not to kill him, to get him out of my head! I can't stand it anymore. I can't have a single solitary thought to myself. Help me break the chain he put on me." I started sobbing halfway through my rant, ending with my face in my hands.

Her gentle touch on my head burned like fire. My sobs turned to screams. "The chains that bind you are the same that bind him. If he has not found a way to chew through them, there is not a god in the nine realms who could aid you. Killing him is the only way to be free and to eliminate the threat to Asgard."

She doesn't want to help me. She wants to help herself.

"No. By helping *you* I am helping the clan of gods who made me one of their own."

Shit. She can hear my thoughts.

"Quite clearly, and I must say that they are not any more organized than your speech."

I hope she can't tell how much I admire her and want to be like her when I grow up. She is the most magnificent goddess I have ever seen, and I bet she could break Fenrir's chains with a snap of her glorious fingers…

"Nice try."

"It was worth a shot."

She reached out and lifted my chin with the tips of her glorious fingers, forcing me to stare into her eyes. "I do see why he picked you. You have more power than you know, and you are quite the little entertainer."

"Amusing or annoying. I get both from different people. Sometimes the same people. Like half and half. Set a trashcan on fire and you get a laugh one day, do it again and they roll their eyes. People are so fickle."

"But not you."

"Nope. One speed. Damn the torpedoes, full speed ahead, Captain Stubing."

"I do not recall any Torpedoes fired at the Love Boat."

Her knowledge of pop culture surprised me. She laughed when I blinked in shock. "You have *cable?*"

She shook her head and closed her eyes for a moment. "It is time. They have healed you and are frantically trying to get you to open those pretty little eyes of yours." She started blinking rapidly, producing a tear in the corner of her eye. She wiped it and put it in my palm. "Just so you know this wasn't a dream," she said and closed my fingers around the tiny sliver of gold. "One last gift from me to you," she whispered and leaned back in, gently kissing me on my forehead. Warmth spread through me, and I closed my eyes, relishing in the feeling. When I opened them, I smiled up at Hiroki. "Hey, foxy."

"Kaede-*sama*," he whispered and collapsed on top of me, sobbing.

∞ ∞ ∞

Gasping, I sat up in bed, alone in the infirmary. At least I was alone in my curtained off area. After Hiroki had collapsed on top of me, I fell asleep stroking his hair. I vaguely recall the frantic voices of the guys, but they were muffled and not really making much sense. The only things that felt remotely real were Hiroki's sobs against my chest and the warmth of the gold in my hand. I didn't even need to look at it to know it was there, or what it meant.

"Hello?" I didn't yell, the pain in my chest wouldn't allow it, but I managed to croak it out loudly enough that the school nurse opened the curtain and blinked at me in surprise.

"You are awake." Lornca gave me a small smile.

"Kinda sorta. My chest hurts though, you got anything for that?"

"I am almost afraid to give you any medication."

"How about a drink?"

She blinked again in surprise. "I see no harm. I have some wine…" She got up and headed for her office.

Sighing, I tried to sit up in my bed, but the pain was almost overwhelming.

That should suffice to teach you to be more careful. I am surprised you survived.

Don't get all choked up over it or anything.

Fenrir snorted in my head. *It was your own stupidity that put you in danger.*

Hey! She literally came at me out of nowhere. There was nothing I could have done. Nobody could have stopped her.

You could have.

Uh, I was turned around.

When you bested her in battle? You should have taken her life. It would have been the honorable thing to do, and you would not have almost died from your lack of foresight.

My hindsight isn't much better than my foresight. Can you shush now? Everything hurts.

Should I not offer to heal you?

They did. I'm put back together, but everything still hurts.

Do you wish to be made whole once again?

No hurty?

58

No pain, he answered with a chuckle.

Maybe. Can I try the wine first? See if that works?

No.

Thunder boomed outside the infirmary windows, or maybe it was just in my head. Either way, my ears were ringing, and I lost vision in my left eye as the white walls illuminated around me. Lornca came running through the curtain, stopped, and dropped the bottle of wine she'd been carrying. The bottle shattered against the ground, splashing red liquid over her bare legs and shooting glass across the room.

Without taking her eyes from me, she reached in her pocket and pulled out an ordinary looking, gray stone and held it palm up before her. I braced for the blast, but she simply spoke to it. "Headmaster to the infirmary, please."

"You have rocks for intercoms?"

She nodded, unable to even blink.

"What?"

Shaking her head slightly, she walked over to the nightstand table beside my bed and opened the drawer, pulling out a hand mirror. She held it out in front of my face, and my fingers swept up, running over my skin to feel for the glowing blue tattoos in the mirror. Of course, I couldn't feel them, but the light was blocked wherever I touched. Even my eyes were glowing, as well as the chain around my neck. I'd seen them once before, and they faded after time. I just hoped they faded again.

No, they will not. Fenrir's voice chuckled in my head.

"Fuck. At least my chest doesn't hurt." I nodded appreciatively as I stretched my shoulders, testing my newly healed flesh.

The door to the infirmary burst open, and Tatsuo skidded to a stop just inside the doorway, my father trailing in behind him. He took one long look at me, closed his eyes and swallowed, and ran across the room. A hit, a slap, maybe some finger shaking. I didn't know what to expect. Wrapping his arms around me and sobbing was the absolute *last* fucking thing in the universe I'd ever imagined. He even repeated my name over and over as he held me and shook. I blinked at Uncle, helplessly. He just smiled.

"Father?"

My uncertainty brought him back to reality. He let go immediately, standing and straightening his clothes, wiping his eyes on the back of his hand. "You are awake."

"*Hai.*"

"When the nurse called, I feared the worst. I am relieved you are all right."

"What happened?" Uncle Tatsuo asked the nurse, not me.

"She woke up, complaining about pain. I went to get her something, and when I came back, she was no longer in pain and covered in runes."

"Just my face," I said defensively.

"Daughter, look at your arms and legs…"

I looked down and cursed under my breath. My hands were free, but tiny little Viking axes and other glyphs completely covered me. I looked like an Icelandic raver princess. "Seriously? How the hell am I supposed to sleep? I'm a *kami*-damned night light."

Uncle Tatsuo chuckled softly but stopped as soon as my father turned and glared. "It faded the last time."

"I'm not so sure this time," I said, not wanting to tell them what Fenrir had said. Or that he was even talking to me still. I sure as shit wasn't going to mention Freya. Or think about her.

"Only time will tell," Tatsuo answered, nodding solemnly.

You wish to not glow?

Uh… Duh.

Find me…

Glow, it is.

One way or another, Little Fox, you shall do my bidding.

You forgot to say, "Muhahahaha."

I do not understand.

60

Nevermind. But blackmailing isn't cool. You're supposed to make me want *to do your bidding. Not force me into it. That's just evil and pisses me off, making me want to do the opposite of what you want. Evil. Eviiiiil.*

I shall impart unto you great wisdom. There is no evil. There is no good. There is only desire.

Desire?

A man kills his brother for his gold. Another man kills his brother to save the life of his wife. One has just reasons. One does not. But no matter the reason, both are dead.

That just hurt my head.

Fenrir's sigh hurt it even more. When the room came back into focus, all three of my visitors were staring at me with a look of something much greater than worry. Maybe fear. "What?"

"You stopped glowing," my father said in relief, but he was still staring at my face.

"Well that's good," I breathed out the breath I hadn't realized I'd been holding. Until I noticed my father still staring at me. "What?"

He took the mirror still in Lornca's hand and held it up for me to see.

The runes weren't glowing, but they were still there. Faint and gray, almost like a tattoo. Just the twin axe runes on my face, the rest were gone. "Well, I guess it is better than looking like a glowstick."

"They are almost…pretty. I do not care for their significance, but they are hardly noticeable."

It was Fenrir's attempt at a compromise. I could live with that. *Thank you,* I whispered to him, meaning it.

I shall leave you to your guests. Make no mistake, you will come find me.

I'm more inclined to do so now. I wasn't lying, either. I still wasn't going to do it, but the odds of it happening did increase one-millionth of one percent. If I had to choose finding him or gouging out my eyeballs with a rusty melon baller and then rinsing the wound with yak spunk, I might go look for him with sunglasses and a blindfold.

"Kaede," Tatsuo started, sighing before he continued, "it is dangerous to keep conversing with him. The more interaction and stimulation he has, the more he wakes."

"You're preaching to the choir, *Oji*." I smiled at him. I hadn't called him *Oji*, the Japanese word for uncle, since I was a little girl. "He keeps talking to me, trying to force me to go to Helheim and find his body. The glowing runes were his latest ploy."

"You must not!" Lornca sounded almost panicked.

"Really? I shouldn't? 'Cause I was just about to go to Helheim, you know, where that other god who hates my guts and wants me dead, lives. Was just about to go grab a taxi…"

"My apologies."

I looked back at my uncle and my father. "Seriously, if you two can do something about Mr. Chatty, I'm all ears. But I can promise you I'm doing the best I can." I gulped internally, thankful I couldn't share Freya's plan with them. Not that I was going to go through with that, *either*. I couldn't kill a mouse, let alone a wolf. Or a god. Or a wolf god. "Well, dying takes a lot out of a girl. Think I'm gonna grab a snack and head to bed."

I stood up to leave and six hands pushed me back down. "You aren't leaving." Lornca was the first to get the words out.

"Uh… He healed me. I'm fine now."

"I'll be the judge of that after a few days of recuperation."

She didn't know me very well. The odds of me sitting in bed for two days doing absolutely nothing were about as good as me charging into hell to free Fenrir.

"Sure, Doc," I said and popped to the other side of the room, waving and slipping out the infirmary door.

"Let her go," Uncle Tatsuo said with a chuckle.

Chapter 6

"Are you sure?"

I looked at Hiroki and nodded. "I feel *fine*. What am I supposed to do all day? Sit in our room and do absolutely nothing until they serve lunch?"

"No. You would get into way too much trouble. Maybe you should accompany me. But you are not to lift anything heavier than the weight of your good judgement."

"I don't have any good judgement."

"Precisely." He knocked my hands away from the buttons of my white shirt and slowly started to do them up, one by one. I grinned at him the whole time and kept twisting, touching his hands with my boobs.

"You getting distracted? Huh? Huh?"

"You are going to need more than that to distract me, Kaede-*sama*."

I gasped. "Did you just say I have itty bitty titties?"

His eyes widened, and he stared at me in contrite dismay. "Kaede-*sama*, I would never! I meant that it would take more than…" He trailed off, finally realizing I was teasing him.

Grinning, I reached out and caressed the front of his pants. "Something like this, perhaps?"

"*Hai*. That would do it." He fumbled with a button. "But please refrain. You are the one who wished for food before class. We will not make it to breakfast."

"Hmmm. Might have to find something here to suck on then. I'm suuure you could find something to *eat*."

He fumbled with the last button, ignoring me completely. "Had you not returned to the room last night complaining of starvation, I might be more inclined to feast upon your flesh and let you devour me. Perhaps *after* class. *If* you behave yourself."

Oh, it's game on now, bitch. I saw it as a moral imperative to make him bust a nut before the end of Home Ec. Maybe even *in* Home Ec. Whip up a fresh batch of man chowder when Professor Shfinkterheim wasn't looking.

"Okaaay." I smiled and handed him my tie. When he upturned my collar, I licked his hand and then placed a gentle kiss on the other, stepping into his arms. "Would it be easier if I turned around?"

Without waiting for an answer, I did just that, holding my hands behind my back and leaning against his chest. Sighing, he put the tie around my neck and leaned over my shoulder to see. My hands bumped against his groin, and he shifted. When he was halfway through the knot, I cupped him and gave him a gentle squeeze, smiling as I felt him harden.

"*Kaede*-sama…"

"Yes, Roki-*kun*?"

He didn't answer, merely finished tying my tie while I stroked him. He was fully hard by the time he finished and had my collar straight. He was good. But I was better. It was going to be a fun day.

He turned and headed for the door, tossing me my jacket and getting the door. We emerged at the same moment as the twins. "You're up early," Romy said in surprise.

"I'm hangry. Figured some breakfast would do a body good."

He nodded and gave me the once over. "I can't believe you're going to class today." It had to be Remy. He sounded impressed with me, and that was something that never happened with Rome.

"Yep. Roki's making me go. He was afraid I'd get in trouble left on my own."

"Wise man. You sure you're feeling okay?"

Rome on the other hand, was staring at the front of Roki's trousers beside me. "I think she's fine," he said with a chuckle and gave Roki a thumbs up.

"Down boy," I said and pushed down on his erection. It sprang back up.

I crossed the hall and raised up on my tiptoes to plant a firm one on Remy. His hand wrapped around my back and pulled me in for that kiss. By the time he was finished, Roki wasn't the only one with a party going on in his pants.

"You better kiss me like that, too," Rome wiggled his eyebrows.

Rome never wiggles his eyebrows. Fuck. Oh, well. When in Rome... Snicker. I moved over to the other twin and kissed him just as hard, if not harder, than his brother.

"Happy now?"

"Quite."

"Can we get some food?"

"David is meeting us there."

"Yay! Let's go."

The four of us headed for the Dining Hall. Roki wasn't the only one having difficulty walking, either. Smiling, I watched them struggle.

The smell of bacon drove all thoughts of sausage from my brain, and I practically ran the last few hundred feet to the dining hall. It was the first time I'd gotten up early enough for breakfast since we started school. I was more of a drink until I pass out, barely make it to class, kind of girl. If I'd known about the all you can eat bacon, I might have struggled once or twice to make an appearance. Because bacon.

"Coffee, too?" I sniffed the air and drooled on my sleeve as I pulled the door open.

"Kaede, what is on your face?" The twins were both staring at me. In the dimly lit hallway of the dorms, they hadn't noticed. My new sporty tattoo wasn't as visible as when I stood in direct sunlight. The entrance to the Dining Hall faced east.

"What? This old thing?" I pointed at my cheeks. "It's been there foreverrr. Can't believe you just noticed." I ignored their dumbfounded looks and went inside, not stopping until I had a tray, plate, and silverware in my hand and was horning in on the tray of bacon.

"Why did you lie about it?" Roki bumped me in the line, pretending to fill his plate with fruit. Who puts fruit next to the bacon? That had to break some sort of cross-contamination rules. Wouldn't want any of that healthy shit spilling over on the salted pork goodness.

"Lie about what?"

"You know what I am talking about. What is wrong with you? You can't even talk to me anymore?"

I sighed and added another five pieces of bacon to my plate out of frustration. It was definitely going to be an angry eat kind of day. "I don't want anybody to worry about me."

"We are your lovers, Kaede-*sama*. We will worry more if you keep things from us."

"I told *you* about it."

"Only after I noticed it last night when you came home."

"I would have said something." I put some chocolate chip pancakes on my plate out of spite.

"When?"

"Sometime."

"Kaede…"

And there it was. He was frustrated and *finally* dropped the honorific. If I'd known it was that simple, I would have upped my frustration game long go. "Drop it, Roki."

I walked away and found a corner table large enough to seat all of us. I was into my sixth piece of bacon when Hiroki set a cup of coffee and a glass of OJ in front of me.

"Fanks," I mumbled around my food.

"I am sorry."

"No, you're not."

"You are correct." At least he grinned at me, but that was Hiroki. He loved me, but when I reached the peak of petulance, he snarked and then apologized. It's how I knew when I was cut off. One time, when I was much younger and full of life, I tested those limits. He suggested weapons practice to blow off some steam. It was a quick lesson on when to stop.

Surprisingly enough, those lessons only had to do with the lines of communication between us. With everything else he had the patience of a saint. I could get drunk, start a bar fight, get arrested, and then verbally abuse the genetic lineage of every cop it took to taser me, and he wouldn't bat an eyelash. I'd never started a bar fight. Technically. The bitch in green fishnets threw the first punch.

Romy set a little pitcher of warm syrup on my tray beside my pancakes, and then put a dish of butter on the table in front of me. I blinked up in surprise. Whichever twin it was, that was sweet. And I'm not talking about the syrup. "Thank you. I forgotted."

"Just don't get killed again, and we'll call it even." It had to be Rome.

"Thanks, Rome."

He just nodded, and Roki winked. I'd gotten one right. Smiling, I dumped the quarter stick of butter on my little happy stack and then doused it, and my bacon, in syrup. Grabbing my fork and knife, I went to pleasure town, making little *mmm*, *mmmm* noises as I chowed. When I finally looked up, four sets of eyes were watching me eat with a look somewhere between fascination and amusement. I hadn't even noticed Remy or David sit down.

"Hi," I said and smiled, mouth full of food.

"Glad to see you're feeling…alive." David's face contorted in a frown.

"Can't keep a pesky fox down. How are *you* feeling?"

"Better. Stronger."

"Faster? Friskier?"

"Kaede, I just have to say, and I'm sure I speak for everyone at this table, please…don't *ever* let anything like that happen to you again. We thought we lost you, and they had to call school security to drag us from your room last night."

I nodded, not knowing what to say. My eyes got a little watery as I took a sip of coffee to clear my throat. "I'll order an anti-stabby vest off Amazon after class."

"Not funny," Rome huffed. "We need to come up with a plan to keep you safe. Sabine probably thinks you're dead. Stephanie is nowhere to be found, but she wasn't my sister's *only* friend. It's only a matter of time until she learns the truth and tries again."

When he put it that way, I wasn't very hungry anymore. But bacon. I kept nibbling and thinking.

When you are in danger, you will know. I blinked in surprise at Fenrir's voice in my head. He had been silent all morning.

How?

He must have gone back to sleep, because he didn't answer.

The four of them stared at me while I stared off into space, waiting for that answer.

"What did he say?" Roki knew the look on my face.

"That I would know if I was in danger from now on."

"Before or after you are a Kaede-kabob?" David slammed his fork down on his tray.

68

I giggled at the Kaede-kabob. I'd use that line again, next time I was impaled on him. That should cheer him up.

"It's not funny, Little Fox."

"No. I was laughing at the kabob part. Trust me, getting skewered isn't fun. With a knife."

The four of them just rolled their eyes and gave up.

∞ ∞ ∞

I stared warily at Professor Welheim. She was at the podium in the front of the class, looking like she was about to drop the bomb on us. She only stood at the pulpit to deliver bad news or voice her frustrations with a certain kitsune to the rest of the class. She was smiling, so I knew her news had to be epically bad of biblical proportions. Everyone else in the class was chatting normally, unawares that life as we knew it was about to end in a cloud of hungry locusts.

"Class… I have some news."

Everyone shut up, and I braced myself on my stool. Roki could feel my fear and patted my leg soothingly. "We're dead. We're all dead."

"I'm sure it is nothing drastic, Kaede-*sama*."

"Rivers turning to blood. No! A meteor shower."

"It is unusual this late in the school year, but we have two new students joining us for the rest of the year! Please welcome Fress and Kottr." She stepped back from the podium, and the two new students stepped into the classroom.

I gasped a little, recognizing them instantly. They were the two admirers that Roki had insisted were checking out my assets on the dance floor. The ones that looked obscenely alike without being twins. At least I would be able to tell them apart. I was more than a little shocked that

69

they had ended up at Aesir Academy. I recognized their names from somewhere, but where eluded me.

"Hello. I am Fress," the blue haired one spoke up and smiled at everybody.

"And I am Kottr." The gray haired one's voice was a lot deeper than Fress', but their accents were identical. And Nordic.

"We are pleased to meet all of you," Fress finished, and they looked to the professor.

"Take the empty table in the back, boys. Today is free cooking, so make whatever you can. Ask any of the other students for help if you need anything."

"Ja. Thank you, Professor."

They took the long way and walked right by Roki and me. They both nodded at us as they passed. Kottr even winked.

"Was that for you or me?" I was unsure.

"I believe you. Would you mind if it was for me?"

"Yes. I'll claw his eyes out. You're mine. Snarl."

Roki chuckled and reached down to turn the oven on.

"What we making today?"

"I was thinking of a salmon souffle for some reason."

"Uh. Okay. Do random foods just pop in your head?"

"Almost as often as nonsensical ramblings appear in yours."

"Woah. You poor thing."

"Please remember, Kaede-*sama*. The *key* to a successful souffle is silence."

"Whelp. There goes our grades. Maybe we should make salmon pancakes?"

"You may whisper."

"Oh. Okay. What we need from the cooler? I'll go get it."

"No. I will. You watch the oven pre-heat."

"Boring."

"Actually, perhaps you should accompany me. I do not wish to leave you alone, either. Not near an open flame."

"Hey. I've been *good* lately. Made that soup all by my lonesome the other day."

"You cut your fingers in seven distinct places."

"Noticed that, did you?"

"I miss very little."

"Except my undying love for you that I harbored all those years."

"You are mistaking ignoring for ignorance."

"Ouch. Thou hast cleft my tiny little heart in twain."

"Please do not use the word undying or the phrase involving the cleaving of your heart again. Ever." He glared at me.

I blushed in embarrassment. My joke having hit a little too close to home for comfort. "Ooops. Sorry."

"You are forgiven. Shall we make our way to the cooler?" He motioned to the back of the room, where the entrance to the gigantic walk-in cooler and freezer the home economics class shared with the Dining Hall was.

"You just wanna see my nipples get hard."

"You are wearing too much padding for me to get a good show."

"Yeah, well. Gotta make 'em look bigger somehow."

"No. You do not." He stopped and took a step closer, lowering himself until his eyes were level with mine. "They are perfect. There is not one part of you that needs to be bigger, smaller, or different. You are absolutely perfect, Kaede-*sama*. All of you, and I mean inside and out."

He blushed, and my eyes juiced up like someone had switched my Visine with lemon drops. I took that last step separating us, grabbed his blazer between my thumb and forefinger, and lowered my head, pressing it into his chest. I kind of wanted to stay there forever, but we had a souffle to cook. And we were getting "Awwws" from the rest of the class.

"Please save your displays of affection for after class, Miss Tanaka and Mister Nishimura."

"*Hai*," Roki answered for me and stepped back. "Come Kaede-*sama*. You can pick out the salmon."

"Okey dokey, Hiroki." I wiped my eyes on the sleeves of my blazer, looked up at him, and smiled.

He motioned toward the cooler door again, and I stopped short. The transfer students hadn't moved an inch and were staring at the two of us intently, heads tilted in opposite directions.

"Uh… Hi? Welcome to Aesir Academy," I said with a hint of a small smile, ignoring the creepy vibe coming off them like cheap aftershave.

"You remember us," Fress said without making it a question.

"Yerp. We saw you in the club the other day."

He nodded and didn't say anything else about it. "You are procuring food for your assignment?"

"Um…yes?"

"Would you show us?"

"Oh," I said in relief. "Sure, follow us. This is Hiroki," I pointed over my shoulder. "And I'm–"

"Kaede," he answered before I could get my name out.

"Woah. How did you know my name?"

Hiroki stepped a little closer to me and slipped his hand against my back, just a gentle reassurance that he was there. A thousand words were conveyed through that gesture.

"We were transferring here when we saw you in the club," Kottr said in his deep, husky voice. "We recognized the uniform and knew you were a student here. When we were getting our class schedules, we asked about you. It would seem most of the faculty knows your name." He coughed a little laugh and quickly covered his mouth with his fingers, embarrassedly.

"Oh. Yeah. I get that."

"We thought it would be nice to find someone who knew the school well, and as luck would have it, you were in our class."

Between the accent and the salted caramel texture of his voice, I found myself relaxing in its almost purred warmth. He should get into radio, but he had a face for TV. They both did.

I held out my hand. "Nice to meet you both."

Fress shook first, and I blinked at the warmth from his hand. It was hot, but not sweaty. Dry, almost too dry. Kottr's was the same. Whatever they were, they had the same vibe.

Hiroki wrapped his arm around me and held it out for them to shake. They both nodded in greeting, and I was jostled as their handshakes with him were a little more manly.

"Come on. Let's go food shopping."

"Shopping?"

"Yeah, the cooler is like a veritable market. Grab a basket when you walk in."

I led the way, Roki right on my ass, and Hanz and Franz flanking us on either side. Once we were inside, I picked up a basket and handed it to Kottr, since he was closer. I grabbed another one for us, but it was snatched from my hand by a stern looking Hiroki.

"No," he muttered softly.

I played the part of the mature kitsune and stuck my tongue out at him. "Think you guys can handle it? Let me know if you need anything." I gave the transfers a little wave and headed for the fish section. The salmon pulled from the waters around the school were amazing, better than any you could find in California, and I was determined to find the best piece the school had to offer.

Master?

The unfamiliar female voice in my head stopped me in my tracks. There was only one girl who called me master in the entire school. Or planet. *Geri?*

Where are you?

Home Ec. What's wrong? Even if I couldn't hear the fear in her voice, I could feel it through our link, slithering down the tendril that connected us like an oily serpent.

Be careful! I'm not positive, but I swear I just saw Sabine...

Her fear became my fear as my chest clenched, and my heart threatened to stop beating. Maybe it was just the memory of the feel of ten inches of icy steel piercing my chest and heart. Either way, I couldn't draw in my next breath as panic seized every muscle in my body.

She is near. I can taste her anger. The last thing in the universe I needed was Fenrir's confirmation.

The walk-in cooler was dimly lit, but everything took on an eerie sheen and sharpened into focus. My heart started beating again, but faster than I'd ever felt it. My limbs went numb and my katana appeared, clenched tightly in my white-knuckled fist.

This is a good blade. Hand axes would be more suited for you, Little Fox.

Uh… Whatcha doin?

Keeping you safe, as promised.

"Miss Tanaka! All of the fish have already been prepped. There is no need for you to have a *sword*. Put that away this instant!"

My head turned, and I focused on Professor Welheim. Fenrir was still at the wheel, though. "This is not for fish, woman. This is for protection."

74

Her eyes narrowed, and the hands on her hips dropped in amazement at the deep unearthly voice that had erupted from my throat. Everything around me started pulsing with blue light, and I knew my tattoos were glowing in time with my heart.

"Protection from whom?"

The air erupted in a flurry of movement behind me. Fenrir duck and spun the moment the first ripple hit the back of my neck, sweeping out with the blade.

Sabine had never stepped from her pocket dimension, so the blade passed ineffectually through the air beneath her outstretched arm. Unfortunately, she had given up on stabbing me.

I wish it was the first time I had stared down the barrel of a gun, but there had been one other time on a trip to LA that will be forever engrained into my memories. It is not a pleasant experience, and not one I would like to have repeated. But there I was.

I could feel Fenrir's confusion. He had no idea what the weapon was, let alone what it could do to my tiny frame. Hopefully I didn't end up looking like a hunk of swiss cheese.

Move! She's got a gun.

I do not know what that is…

Fires projectiles. A hundred times faster than arrows!

Oh.

She pulled the trigger, and I tried to close my eyes for what I was sure was going to be the very last time. They didn't budge, and time slowed around me as Fenrir lifted us up from our crouch and batted the bullet aside with the flat of my katana.

I could feel his sense of pride.

It shoots more. A lot more.

The muzzle erupted in fire again, catching Fenrir off guard. The slug hit my shoulder, and blood blossomed through my blazer. Luckily, it wasn't the shoulder holding the blade. His pride turned to embarrassment as the pain hit me. He didn't feel a damn thing, the bastard.

My apologies. I thought she would have to rearm her weapon. I have never seen such a wondrous thing! You must get some.

Don't like guns, I answered through gritted mental teeth as I fought for control of my body to cradle the arm hanging limply at my side.

Out of the corner of my eye, I saw Roki round the corner of one of the sets of metal shelves dividing the cooler. He was twenty feet away, and I wanted to scream at him to stop, but just like the rest of me, my mouth belonged to Fenrir. *That sounded really dirty.*

Roki ran in slow motion, calling his katana as the gun went off three times in Sabine's hand, visible just past her wrist as the rest of her was snuggled safely in another world. *Cheating bitch.*

She fights like a coward, Fenrir said to me.

An effective coward. I had to stab into her pocket space to get her the last time.

I see. I felt him combing through my memories and shuddered. Fenrir had done all that in the space it took for the three bullets to travel to me. Roki had just begun to scream my name as he blocked the first bullet that had been on a trajectory to splatter my insides level with my belly button. I knew he had no chance against the other two. The bullet hit the blade and deflected off behind me and to the left. I just hoped there wasn't anybody behind me.

Two spheres of glowing gold erupted in front of the other two bullets before they could get to me, and immediately sensing the respite, Fenrir launched my sword at the disembodied hand like a spear.

In a completely anti-climactic scene, the sword spun instead of flying true, and the handle hit the gun, knocking it from her hand. Two more glowing spheres flew right after it and exploded just as she pulled her hand through and closed the rift.

Fenrir let go, and I dropped to the ground, groaning in agony.

Thank you, I said softly to him. For all his faults, he had done the best he could and kept me alive, if slightly perforated.

My apologies for your injury. I did not know such weapons existed. Mankind has come a long way.

Not always for the better. I'm alive. For that, you have my thanks.

I felt his mental nod, and then heat erupted from the wound, feeling like someone had set off a volcano in my arm. My groans of pain turned into screams of despair, and then blackness overwhelmed me.

Chapter 7

"Welcome back."

I blinked at the blonde-haired head hovering over me. "Lornca?"

"Aye."

"I'm in the infirmary again?"

"Aye."

I groaned as I sat up, expecting a torrent of pain. When nothing happened, I blinked and rolled my shoulder. There wasn't even a twinge. "Pretty sure I remember getting shot…"

"Aye. Luckily the two new students were with you. They have miraculous healing abilities. You should probably keep them near you at all times," she said with a small chuckle.

"Or, I could just not get shot. Or stabbed."

"Well, I don't see that happening in your near future."

"What day is it?"

"Still Tuesday."

"Did I miss dinner?"

"No."

"Thank fuck."

"Language."

"*Arigato kuso.*"

"Saying it Japanese doesn't make it better." She lightly smacked me in the forehead with her handy dandy clipboard.

"Well, thanks for the bed! I'ma go grub me some sterk."

"Sterk?"

"Steak."

"Kaede…" She set the clipboard down on the counter.

"I feel fine Doc."

"You're changing."

"Like, getting hair in funny places changing?" I laughed at my own joke and stopped short at the face she made. "What?"

"Call your demi-form. I noticed the change when you came in. Parts of you were shifting."

"What?"

"Bring out your tails."

Shrugging I slid off the bed and did just that, chasing them around to get a better look at what she was talking about. "What the ever-loving fuckballs of a motherless goat?" I resisted the urge to scream. Barely.

My pure white tails were tinged slightly gray at the end and straight up the back. And they were floofier. Maybe a bit longer, too? At least there were still nine of them.

"There's more…"

"I can't handle more. This is bad enough!" Reaching into the drawer, I pulled out the mirror she had shown me my tattoos in during my last visit. I breathed a sigh of relief and sat back down on the bed. "At least the hair on my head is still white."

"Shift completely."

"I don't wanna."

"Please. It is important that you understand the gravity of your situation."

"What situation?"

"You will understand when you shift."

Sighing, I stood back up and let my fox out. Lornca seemed much taller from my prone position on all fours, and she squatted before me, grabbing the mirror off my bed and holding it out in front of me.

Ice blue eyes blinked back at me in the mirror. And that was the only thing I recognized. The fur on my back matched my tails, a wide streak of gray running the length and branching out over my tails. The fur on my face had a mask of gray, too. I wasn't a wolf, but I didn't look entirely fox, either. Like some weird hybrid. I looked like a fucking husky. Huskitsune? Kitsky?

I whined pitifully at Lornca, begging her to take away the mirror. In a fit of depression, I leapt onto the bed, spun in three circles, and plopped down on the mattress, putting my larger snout between my paws.

"It's okay, Kaede."

I growled.

"I'm sure once the chains are broken, you'll be back to your normal foxy little self."

"Easy for you to say," I mumbled through my long jaws, my larger canines threatening to pierce my tongue while trying to form words. That was the last thing I needed. Father was already going to flip his fox lid if he saw my new form. A tongue piercing might cause irrevocable mental damage.

"You are drawing too close to him. He is a wolf. Try and limit your contact as much as possible. It will probably slow the change."

"Probably?" That's what I was trying to say, but the word that filtered through my face was almost unintelligible. I should have picked an easier one. I had trouble saying "probably" with a human mouth.

At least Lornca understood me. "Yes. Probably. You are sailing in uncharted waters. I suggest you stick to the shallows."

"Doggy paddle?"

She smiled at my joke. For the first time. "Yes."

I shifted back and sat crisscrossed on the mattress. "He took over my body when Sabine attacked. If it weren't for him, I'd be dead."

"I am not saying you shouldn't show him gratitude, just limit your conversations. The more you interact with him, the faster the change will come, and the faster he will wake."

"Tell *him* that. He's like a peanut gallery."

I do not understand that term? What is a peanut?

Ignoring him, I made a shushing noise at Lornca and pointed at my ear. She nodded in understanding. In a fit of brilliance, I grabbed her clipboard off the counter and motioned for her to hand me her pen out of her lab coat pocket. Flipping over the page, I hastily scrawled, *He's listening, but I don't think he can read. If you want to say mean things about him, write it down.*

She nodded.

"Well, I need to get some food into me. Getting shot takes a lot out of a girl. Need to replace those holes with some beef."

"Okay, but if you feel ill, come back to the infirmary. If I'm not here, the night nurse will be."

"Thanks, Lornca." I gave her a quick hug, ignoring the fact that she totally stiffened when I did, and headed for the door. Stopping just before the exit, I turned back around and stared at her thoughtfully. "Hey, Lornca?"

"Yes?"

"This changing stuff… Did anybody else see it?"

"Hiroki and the two new students were there when you started shifting. Hiroki may have noticed, but I don't think the other two would have thought anything of it. Why?"

"It stays between us, okay?" If she told Tatsuo, he might mention it to my father. That was the last fucking thing in the universe I needed.

"Nurse-patient privilege. I'm not allowed to discuss your health with anybody but you."

"*Kami* bless HIPAA."

She actually chuckled. "Be careful, Kaede."

"I'll just be happy if somebody captures Sabine. That stabby, shooty little bitch needs to go."

Lornca's eyes narrowed, and she nodded solemnly.

I opened the door to the infirmary and left, skidding to a stop outside the door. Roki, David, Remy, *and* Rome were all pacing outside the door. "Uh… Hey?"

They all spun and surged toward me like a masculine tidal wave of sexy. I got lost in the hug that ensued, and I'm not gonna lie, I fucking liked it. By the time they pulled away, I was grinning like an idiot. Don't get me wrong, I did a *lot* of things like an idiot, but I don't think I'd ever been happier in my life than I was at that moment. "It's like you missed me or something."

Roki dropped to the ground in front of me, bowing his head. "Kaede… I failed you."

"No, you didn't. And don't ever let me hear you say stupid shit like that again. That's my job."

He looked up at me, tears streaking down his cheeks. He seriously blamed himself. "I should not have left you alone."

"I should have called for you. Geri saw Sabine and warned me the minute she did. I froze. My fault."

"Geri saw her?" Romy's eyebrows knit.

"Yeah. Why?"

"I know of Sabine's talent for traversing dimensions. While I did not know she possessed the talent, it is known among our clan. It takes a vast amount of magic to maintain. She cannot simply wander the school undetected. She had to traverse to *where* you were and *then* shift. Wherever you are, you will be guarded *outside* the location. If Sabine comes for you, we should be able to spot her and get you to safety."

I blinked in surprise. "That's not a half-bad idea. How is the guard going to warn me?"

"The staff uses two-way radios, and I use that term loosely. They rely on magic instead of technology. I might be able to procure a set or two from the Headmaster."

"You talkin' bout the walkie-talkie rocks?"

"You've seen them."

"Yep. Lornca called for the Headmaster on one."

"I'll go speak to him now."

"Avoid my father if you see him."

Rome, and there was no doubt it was him with his take charge attitude, nodded. He seemed angry. I wasn't sure if it was at me or his sister. "I'll find you after I speak with the headmaster."

"Don't look too hard. I'll be eating."

That earned me a smile. He looked at Roki and narrowed his eyes before he left, communicating silently.

"What was that?" As soon as Rome was gone, I had to ask. The exchange worried me.

"Rome was less than happy that Sabine had managed not only to find out that you were still alive, but to attack you again within a day." Remy ran his fingers through his hair and leaned against the wall.

"He blames Roki?" That pissed me off. If I didn't blame him, Rome had no reason to, either.

"No. He blames Sabine. But he wasn't too happy with your bodyguard for not guarding your body. He yelled at him for moving more than five feet away from you."

"And if he had been closer, he would have died. He didn't have a Fenrir to take over his body and slash bullets out of the air."

All three of them stared at me uncertainly.

"I had wondered how you did that." Roki nodded, finally understanding. He and I needed to have a long talk. Especially about anything he might have seen with my uncontrolled shifting.

"Yeah. I was on autopilot. Where are the new kids? I need to thank them for their help. And for healing me."

The three of them looked at each other, and another moment of silent communication passed between them.

"What?"

It was David who finally spoke. "Do you know them?"

"Other than seeing them in the club the other night, and having class with them today, no. Why?"

"They seem to know a lot about you. Including what you are. When you were shot, they were working over you like a pair of EMTs. What would work, and what wouldn't, on your kitsune heritage. They were even mumbling about mutations in the DNA chains and a whole bunch of stuff none of us understood. They even called your father by name when they thought you were going to need a blood transfusion."

"They know my father?"

"His name at least. You don't think he sent them in to protect you, too, do you?"

"No. I don't think he knew how much danger I was in until yesterday. They were here before that. Maybe Uncle Tatsuo hired them?"

The three of them shrugged. Anything was possible with the mysterious dragon. Then I realized something.

"How do you all know this?"

"Geri. She was practically plowing through everybody to get to you. And then when you were shot, she went down screaming in the middle of the hallway. Rome, Remy, and I were there. She told us to find you. We made it in time to see Kotter and Fress ripping your shirt off." He chuckled.

"That's funny?"

"No, but Remy not knowing they were trying to *heal* you, was. They almost got decapitated."

I looked over at a very embarrassed Remy, leaning against a wall, and looking *everywhere* but at me. "Awww." I snickered.

"I'll apologize again."

"I'm sure they understand."

"So, what were they talking about DNA mutations for? Do you know?" David seemed curious.

"Nope. Not a clue. Come on, let's get some dinner."

"You want to change first?"

I looked down and laughed. With everything that had been going on, I hadn't even noticed what I was wearing. Or I was getting used to wearing it. "Yeah. Hospital gown isn't very chic. Where's my clothes?"

"Unsalvageable. Your blazer had a huge hole in it and was covered in blood. Your shirt they tore into wads to stop the bleeding until they could heal you."

"My entire tuition is probably going to uniform replacements."

"I doubt you have gone through three million dollars' worth of uniforms," David said with a chuckle. He stared at me when I turned white. "What?"

"Three million?" I gulped audibly

"Yeah. You didn't know?"

All I could do was shake my head. No wonder my parents were so disappointed in me. Sure, they had the money, but holy fuck. That was a lot of rice.

Shaking my head, I looked up at them. "Do I have time to take a shower?"

They smiled and nodded. Except for Hiroki. He hadn't gotten over my getting shot on his watch. I didn't know whether to give him some time to start believing it wasn't his fault, or smack him with a wet noodle until he got it through his thick skull. I was going to have to keep an eye on him.

"Great. Let's go. There should be room for all four of us." I grinned over my shoulder.

"Rome's going to be pissed he missed this." Remy chuckled.

Chapter 8

"Okay, I'ma be honest. This is *not* what I had in mind." I rinsed the shampoo out of my hair and stuck my tongue out at Remy's and David's backs. Roki was in the hall *outside* the bathroom, and the other two were guarding the stall I was showering in. They weren't even watching the naked Kaede show.

"You were just shot. Clean now, food next, play later." Remy's voice left little room for argument.

"Boring."

"What was that?" He glanced over his shoulder.

I held up the bottle of shampoo. "No sting. That's what the package said, but my eyes are burning a little."

"Come here."

I practically skipped to the edge of the shower stall, thinking he was caving. He turned around, cupped my chin in his strong fingers, and stared into my eyes. "They're not red, but we shouldn't take any chances."

Leaning in, I closed my eyes and felt him gently kiss my right eyelid and then my left. I practically melted in his hand, and I smiled when he finished. The kiss on my lips was totally unexpected, and I had to fight the urge to wrap my naked wet self around him.

"Woah," I whispered when he let go of me.

"Not so boring, am I?"

"You did hear me."

"Yes."

"Wanna join me?"

"After dinner." He winked.

Growling in frustration, I turned around and shut the water off. Grabbing my towel and robe, I burst through the two of them, stomping off toward my room and ignoring Roki as I passed by him.

"What did you do?" I heard him ask the two of them as they came out of the bathroom.

"Told her no," Remy said defensively.

"Yes, that would do it." Roki chuckled.

I was halfway down the hallway when Kottr and Fress walked out of their room, stopped, and stared at me. There was no way in hell I was going to even acknowledge their presence. Not while I was in the middle of teaching Remy a valuable lesson.

My nerves got the best of me, and I popped to the end of the hall, just outside my door, before realizing I didn't have my key because Roki was with me, and he was the key master. I wanted to scream in frustration and did the only thing I could do... I turned my happy naked ass invisible.

"Where'd she go this time?" Remy looked behind them.

Roki just smirked and sped up, knowing I couldn't keep the invisibility going for more than half a minute. "I hope you have learned your lesson," he whispered as he shoved the key in the door and turned the knob. Stepping back, he let me in the room first.

"Is she in there?" I heard David call out to Roki.

"*Hai,*" he answered and held the door open for the two of them while they caught up.

I dropped the invisibility, practically panting from the exertion. Remy marched through the door and stopped when he saw me. "How the hell did you get in here? Thought you couldn't teleport through doors."

"Can't," I managed to stammer.

"She cannot," Roki translated. "She can, however, turn invisible for a few moments. I had to open the door for her."

David was ignoring the conversation and staring at my nakedness, what wasn't covered by the towel and robe I was holding mostly in front of me. *At least somebody appreciates me.*

Remembering our conversation, I walked over to my dresser, pulled out a pair of panties, and slid them on. I even pulled out a skirt and one of my button-down white shirts. Tossing the skirt on the bed, I slowly put the shirt I put on. Grabbing a pair of socks, I sat down on the corner of the bed, facing everybody. Spreading my legs, I slipped one sock on and looked up with just my eyes to gauge David's reaction. I didn't need to look higher than his belt. He wasn't kidding about his fascination with panties, even white cotton ones. Unable to help myself, I scooted forward just enough to really pull my panties tight against my flesh and pulled my other sock on my foot.

"David, could you hand me my shoes please? They're by the door."

"Uh, yeah. Sure."

When he turned around, I leaned back on my hands, spreading myself even more, and waited for him to turn around. When he did, one shoe fell from his hand. "My shoulder's a little sore, David. Would you mind putting them on for me?"

The gulp was audible. As was the chuckle from Remy.

He knelt in front of me, and I offered him one of my feet, having to hold it there for a long moment until he could tear his eyes from me. "Sorry," he mumbled and started to slip the shoe on my foot, eyes glancing up every other second.

"Should I have covered up first?" I tried to sound as innocent as possible.

91

He wasn't buying my spiel and narrowed his eyes. "You're evil."

"Am I? Isn't this what you like? I thought I was doing something nice for you."

"You are. But you're also tempting me, and I'm pretty sure that classifies as evil."

I spread my legs a little further. "Give into your lust, David. Join the dark side. We have nookies."

Sighing, he pulled off the shoe he's just put on and let it drop to the floor beside him. Leaning forward, he ran his lips ever so gently over the gusset of my panties. "You win."

"I do."

"I'm pretty sure I do, too."

"Really? She flashes you her underwear and you cave?" Remy didn't sound disgusted, more amused.

"I know his kryptonite." I grinned at him. "Don't worry, I'll figure out yours, too. Bwahaha."

"Fox Luthor." He chuckled and pulled off his shirt. I tried to stare at his gorgeous frame, but my eyes were crossing from David's tongue gently lapping at me through my panties. He hadn't even bothered to move them out of the way.

"Lay back." Remy pulled a pillow off the head of the bed and put it behind my head. As soon as I did, he leaned over me and his lips met mine. Another set of hands started unbuttoning my shirt. When a third set of lips closed around my nipple, I knew Hiroki had caved, too.

Remy pulled away from the kiss, and I whimpered. "Well, you got what you wanted, fox. We're going to make you sorry."

"Sorry?"

"Yes. We're going to make you come so many times, you won't be able to think straight for a week."

"It's not one of my," I paused to gasp in pleasure as David's tongue slipped behind my panties and inside me, "strong suits, anyway. Thinking straight is highly overrated."

Remy chuckled and teased my other nipple with his fingers. "Tell me what you want."

"Your cock. I want to suck you."

"Do you?" His throaty chuckle turned into a chesty growl as he unbuckled his pants next to me. He didn't take them off, simply unbuttoned them and freed himself. I put my ankles behind David and pulled him in closer as I reached up to wrap my hand around Remy's cock and stroke him.

"Come here," I said and led him closer by tugging him toward me. He crawled forward on his knees until he was right next to my head, his cock dangling tantalizingly over my lips. I planted a gentle kiss just behind the underside of his head, and he groaned. "You want to come in my mouth, Remy?"

He nodded as I pulled him down and suckled the head, running my tongue over the tip and teasing the hole on the end. Tapping Roki on the shoulder, I reached under him as he lifted his head, motioning to his cock. I wanted one in my hand, one in my mouth, and one inside me. Letting go of David with my legs, I pulled Remy from my mouth and lifted my head to look at David. "Fuck me, David."

The two of them shifted, Roki getting on his knees beside me, and David shifting between my legs. This was going to be epic. As soon as Roki's cock was in my hand, I started pumping him and taking Remy back into my mouth. Both of them were smooth as silk, and yet so different. Remy much thicker, but Roki longer and thinner. David was more in the middle of both. They were perfect, and they were mine.

"Slowly, Kaede."

I pulled him from my mouth with a soft *pop* and smiled at him. "Getting close or just want to enjoy?"

"Little bit of both."

David's fingers pulled apart my wet flesh, and I felt the tip of him settle inside. He lifted my legs and wedged his arms under them, giving him the angle he wanted as he slowly slid himself inside me fully.

"Oooh. Yes, please. I needed that."

He smiled at me from above. "Is that what you wanted?"

Nodding, I took Remy back into my mouth, tugging Roki even closer. Two cocks above me and one inside me. Heaven didn't seem so far away.

"You're leaving Roki out," Remy said and ran his fingers through my hair.

"You want me to suck him, too?"

He nodded, with a hungry look in his eye.

Without a word, I pulled him closer and pulled him into my mouth, lifting my head from the pillow and taking damn near all of him. I could feel him throbbing in my mouth, and I started to whimper around him as David began long slow strokes inside me.

I pulled Roki free and sucked Remy for a few moments before going back, alternating between the two of them with my mouth and hands.

"That is so fucking hot," David whispered above me. He had a closeup show of the entire thing, his face very close to mine.

"You want some of this?" I pulled Roki from my mouth and offered him a taste, knowing better than to offer him Remy. I wasn't sure if he would take Roki, but I didn't think Remy would enjoy another man's mouth on *his* cock. Well, he might enjoy the *feeling*, but would probably be way to proud to admit it.

David stared at the cock in front of him for a long moment before looking at me. I gave him a hungry smile. Then he shocked me by looking up at Remy, almost seeking approval. Half expecting Remy to give David a horrified look, instead he nodded. I almost squealed in happiness. Roki pulled himself from my hand and turned, offering himself to David.

Not wanting to miss the show, I ran my lips and tongue on the underside of Remy's shaft and teased the head, not tearing my eyes from the hunger in David's eyes as he slowly pulled Roki to his mouth. Tentatively, he reached out and licked the tip. I wasn't sure what he was expecting, but he widened his eyes in surprise and pulled Roki's tip into his mouth, groaning as he did and pumping himself into me again.

I was on cloud fucking nine.

I wasn't the only one who was more than turned on by the whole situation. "Kaede," Remy made my name a warning.

"Are you going to come?"

He nodded and raised his head in the air, practically fucking my fist with spastic movements of his hips. Instead of taking him back into my mouth, I ran the head of his cock over my lips, licking the tip.

"Holy fuck…" He groaned the words as hot wetness splashed over my mouth and across my cheek. Rubbing him against my face, I let him shoot twice more over my chin and my neck, wanting him to paste it over me. I felt so dirty and hot, it made the feel of David's cock drive me insane with lust.

Remy collapsed next to me, cradling my head against his stomach, his spent cock still somewhat excited. "That was fucking hot," he whispered. "Does David feel good?"

"Yesss," I hissed.

"Are you going to come?"

I nodded, unable to find words. Words were hard.

"Do you want David to come inside you?"

I managed to shake my head, still not safe.

"You're not on birth control?"

Again, I shook my head.

"David…" Remy got his attention with the firmness of his voice. "Don't come in our little fox."

He just nodded with a mouthful of Roki, closing his eyes and enjoying the moment.

"You want him to come all over you again?"

This time, I nodded. Not caring if I needed another shower.

"Roki, too?"

The thought sent a stab of pleasure through me, from my nipples to my clit, and I was about three seconds from coming. A high-pitched noise erupted from my throat as David started plowing into me harder. He was as close as I was.

When he pulled Roki from his mouth and straightened, I knew it was coming. Literally. He grabbed himself and slid up the valley between my lips, nudging my clit as he raised himself and ejaculated all over my stomach. It was more than enough to send me over the edge, and I reached down, finishing what he had started, fingering myself over the edge of oblivion. My orgasm had just peaked when Roki began pumping himself over my breasts, the heat prolonging my agony and intensifying it. I screamed as my eyes rolled and my toes curled.

We all lay there panting. Roki and David had collapsed around me, as well. "Holy shit," I managed to stammer after a moment or five.

"Happy now?" Remy carefully stroked some of my hair plastered to my face off of my cheek.

"No. I'm fucking starving. Can we go eat now?"

It was Roki's hand that smacked my ass. I giggled as I got off the bed and went to find my damp towel.

"Do I have time to take a shower?"

"No!" It was the first time the three of them had seen eye-to-eye on anything.

Chapter 9

"Hi, Kaede," Romy's voice said from behind me.

I screeched and spun, my katana in my hand before I had even realized I'd called it. I managed to stop myself from slicing it across the twin's arm as he instinctively brought it up to defend himself.

"Woah! Easy. It's me."

I dropped the blade and it faded into nothing. Then the tears started falling, and I couldn't stop them. It had been three days since Sabine's last attack, and it was starting to wear on my nerves. Looking for her everywhere had finally taken its toll, and I'd snapped. Standing in the middle of the hall sobbing, I didn't give a shit about the students giving us a wide berth and me disdainful looks.

Hiroki put his hand on my back, offering me his shoulder, but Romy didn't give me a chance. He wrapped me in his arms and held me in the hall. "I'm sorry. I didn't mean to frighten you."

"I know," I said and wiped my face against him. "Can't take this anymore."

"I know," he whispered. "Come on. We're skipping. Roki, can you tell your teacher that Kaede isn't feeling well, and I'm taking her to the infirmary?"

"*Hai.*" I felt Roki's familiar warmth leave its usual spot behind me and focused on the warm hardness in front of me.

"I don't wanna go to the nurse."

"I know. We aren't, but it is a plausible explanation for your teacher."

"Smart man."

"Come on. Let's go."

"Where?"

"You'll see." He pried me away from his chest and took my little hand in his big meaty one. His hands were so different from Roki's there was no familiarity. Even scared half out of my mind, it was a little exciting.

We headed for the main building, and I thought he was full of shit about not going to the infirmary until we made it to the front door. "Wait, what? *Skip*, skip?"

"That's the plan, unless you have some sort of objection?"

"Nope. Get me the hell out of here."

"As you command, my lady," he whispered with a smile.

"Going somewhere, Mr. Lateran? Miss Tanaka?"

We turned and saw the headmaster standing behind us with his arms crossed over his chest. He looked less than happy, and we were *so* busted. "Yes, sir. We are going to the village."

"Understood. Please be careful."

"We will, sir."

My uncle shot me an almost imperceptible nod and turned around, heading for his office.

"Uh, what just happened?"

"The headmaster trusts me."

"And me?"

"Not so much, but you're with me. How much trouble could you possibly get into?"

"Oh, my sweet summer child. Let me show you." I grabbed his hand and pulled him toward the one singular cab waiting outside the school. It was Friday afternoon, and students weren't allowed to leave for the village until after the day's classes were over. He must have been bored and waiting for school to get out. Charon's technically ferried the dead to the afterlife, but they also ferried the students of Aesir Academy to and from school in their down time. Gold coins were gold coins. "Thanks," I said as he opened the door, and I slid into the cab.

"For?"

"Getting me out of there. I was seriously losing my effing mind."

"That mustn't have taken long," he answered with a smile.

"Where to?" The cabby interrupted our conversation, adjusting the mirror so he could see us. I fervently wished he hadn't and looked out the window, letting Romy answer his gruesome visage.

"Oddi, of course. Thank you," he said and handed over a gold coin.

There was a metallic *tink* from the front as he deposited the coin wherever it was charons kept their money. I didn't want to think about it.

"So, what do you feel like doing? Are you hungry?"

"Did you just ask me that? Second lunch sounds delightful."

"As you command, Ms. Frodo." He chuckled and leaned closer to the driver. "Know a good restaurant in the village? Not the pub or fast food."

The cabby nodded without a word. We were in his hands in more ways than one. I mean, he did have the power to ferry us to the underworld if we wanted.

Yes. Come find me.

Maybe later. I'm on a date.

"So, food and?"

"I'll leave it up to you."

Romy nodded. "Wait, you do know which one I am, right?"

That was enough of a clue. "Of course, Rome."

He sighed and shook his head. "Fifty-fifty shot, and you blew it." His laughter filled the enclosed cab.

"I meant Remy. Your names are even too close to tell apart, sometimes."

"Yeah. Being a twin isn't all it's cracked up to be."

"I can see that." I giggled for a moment. "Could you imagine if there were two of *me?*"

"Oh, fuck no. One of you is more than the world can handle."

I snuggled closer to him. "But not you. You can handle me *just* fine, can't you."

"Sometimes." He winked to let me know he was kidding.

"You handled me just fine the other day... Bwahahaha."

He seemed confused for a moment and then remembered. "Oh. Yeah. That was fun."

"Fun? You busted a nut on my face, and all I get is, 'Fun?' You need to broaden your sexual description vocabulary." I elbowed him in the ribs.

"Amazing."

"Better, but still not descriptive enough."

"Fucking amazing?"

"Okay. That's tolerable."

He breathed a sigh of relief and seemed more than a little nervous about something. "We're almost there."

"Yay. Food."

The charon pulled the cab in front of a small brownstone building a couple of blocks off the main street of Oddi. I looked around through the pristinely clean window of the cab at the surrounding buildings and shook my head. No wonder we had never eaten there, there wasn't even a sign. "You're sure this is a restaurant?"

The cabby just nodded, and Remy opened the door, getting out first and offering me his hand. "Come on."

"Shit. I forgot to get the credit card from Hiroki."

"I didn't invite you on a date to let you pay for everything." His eyebrows knit above his beautiful eyes.

"I know. But I hate being a mooch."

He silenced me with a little kiss. "I'll consider that payment for your portion of the bill."

"Did you just call me a whore?"

"What? Wait. No! What the hell, Kaede! I was trying to be sweet."

"I know. Thank you, and I was kidding." I booped his nose and headed for the door.

"Don't do that. You made my heart stop."

"Sorry." I had the sense to blush. "Stuff like that just sort of pops out of my mouth before I can stop it. My lips are faster than my brain."

"What about your tongue?"

"You already know the answer to that."

He snaked around me and grabbed the handle to the large glass door. I caught the name Aegir og Ran. Pretty, but I had no idea what the hell it meant. For all the Icelandic I spoke, we could have just walked into "Cock and Balls."

The smell that wafted over us was incredible. The walls were all wood, but looked like driftwood that had been thinly sliced and painstakingly pieced together like a puzzle and glued to the wall. The floor was the same, but of thicker planks. From the ceiling hung a giant domed half globe of stained glass. Waves, sharks, mermaids, and a thousand other creatures of the sea almost seemed to be swimming through the blue glass. I gasped at the beauty of it.

"Woah. You sure you can afford this place?"

"Yep. It's you I'm not so sure about."

"Oh, you can crack jokes, but I can't?"

"If your jokes involve me calling you a whore, no. You're not. Ever."

I stood up on my tiptoes and pulled his head down to me, since I still had no chance of reaching his face with my lips. He acquiesced, and I pulled him closer, turning his head at the last moment and planting my lips against his, instead of his cheek. Sweetness of that magnitude deserved tongue.

"Now you can get dessert, too," he said with a happy, lazy smile.

"Ohhh. Chocolate."

He laughed as the tallest old person I'd ever seen walked out of the kitchen, wiping his hands on his apron. "Welcome. Table for two?"

"Yes, please," Remy said and nodded.

He motioned for us to follow him, leading us back to a small table in the corner of the tiny restaurant. Surprisingly, we were the only other patrons in the place. "Are we too early for dinner? Is that why we're the only ones here? We can come back later if that would be better?"

He paused and turned, giving me a smile. "No, young lady. We do not get many visitors as we are off the beaten path. Only traffic brought to us from the charons, finds our humble eatery."

"Do you get a lot of students from the Academy?" Remy seemed a little dubious, and I didn't blame him. If the charons recommended a restaurant…

"Some yes, mostly couples like yourselves looking for someplace quiet and a good meal."

Then I noticed he didn't have any accent. He was definitely a supernatural of some sort. "Well, thank you for your hospitality." I gave him a grin.

"May I start you off with something to drink?"

Remy looked at me. "Mead?"

The giant nodded and looked at Remy. "Wine."

"Very good."

"Uh, do you have a menu?" I was curious more than hungry. Needless to say, that meant I was *very* curious.

He shook his head. "No. We serve you food we think you would like."

"What do you think I would like?" I couldn't help but ask.

"It is a surprise. My wife will be by to judge your order." Without another word, he left and headed for the kitchen.

"Curious place."

"It is," Remy agreed nervously.

"Wanna go get some cheekin instead? Your brother found me a KFC the other night."

"He did?"

"Yerp. Best meal I've had since I've been here."

He grinned but then got curiously silent. "Did you enjoy spending time with Rome?"

"Don't tell him, but I do."

"You do?"

"Yeah. He can be moody, dour, and mean, but that's just a front. Underneath his crusty shell, he's actually kind of sweet. Like a candy bar. Crunchy on the outside, ooey and gooey on the inside."

"Do you find him attractive?"

"Uh… I better. I find you attractive."

"True."

He rubbed his chin just as the waiter brought our drinks and set them on the table. He was followed by a woman who was just as tall as he was, but about a thousand times angrier looking. Like we had inconvenienced her by showing up. She stared at Remy for just a moment before settling her gaze on me and giving a little gasp. That wasn't the reaction I'd been hoping for. I'd been hoping for a quick glance and an exclamation of, "French fries!"

"Leave," she said and spun around. The waiter grabbed her arm, keeping her from storming off, and turned her back around. "Ran. We do not turn away guests. No matter whom they serve. Do you have her order?"

"Yes, Aegir."

"Good. Begin," he said and let her go. She stormed off to the kitchen, and I looked at him guiltily.

"We can go? I don't want to upset your cook."

"Wife."

"Or her."

"In three thousand years, we have never turned away a guest. We are not about to start now."

"You know about my condition?"

He nodded.

"Know any way I can get out of it?" If they were that old, maybe they knew something none of the others did.

He bent down and looked into my eyes, the corner of his mouth curving up in half a smile. "Use the gifts given to you. You are now in control of your own fate and that of those around you." He reached out and touched his finger to my forehead.

"What does Seidr mean?"

"It means snare in the old tongue." He looked at the ceiling and spoke in Old Norse. I'd heard some of the words before, but couldn't make out the meaning. "The string of fate is in your hand."

He turned around and left us sitting there. Remy had already polished off half his wine and was staring after the old man. "What was all that about?"

"Beats the hell out of me. What kind of food do you think I'll get?"

"That is what you're worried about?"

106

"Fuck yeah. You don't think she's going to bring me," I paused to lean in and whisper the word, "salad. I can't handle another salad. I had one this week already."

He just chuckled and shook his head. I scooted my chair a little closer to him and leaned my head against his shoulder, grateful for his company.

"So, about Rome. You know he really likes you, right?"

"Yes, but he has a funny way of showing it. I wish he'd just calm his titties and be nicer to me. I am what I am, it's not like I'm going to calm down, stop cracking jokes, and mellow out. Not in my DNA."

"Maybe he doesn't want you to."

"He's got a funny way of showing it."

"He's alpha. Maybe he equates that with being calm, cool, and collected all the time."

"Maybe he should pull the panties from his butt. He needs try to have a little fun."

"Or a little fox?"

I grinned up at Remy. "Yerp. A little fox goes a long way."

"That it does." He smiled and kissed the top of my head.

I sat up, looked into his eyes, and pressed my lips against his. He tensed for a moment but melted into the kiss like chocolate in my hand. Technically, he was getting hard in my hand, I couldn't resist caressing him as we sat there waiting for our food.

"Kaede," he hissed as he pulled away.

"What? There's like nobody in here."

"That's…not."

"Cheekin."

"What did you call me?" He gave a little chortle of disbelief.

"Cheekin. Bwak bwak." I even did the little flappy wing thing with my arms and bobbed my head.

"Don't start something you can't finish, Kaede."

I was reaching for his zipper when he pushed my hand away. "There's something I need to tell you first."

"That you wuv me? Cuz I already know that much."

"No." He sighed and just when he was about to tell me more, the waiter brought out two heaping plates of food. Just the way I liked them.

"Saved by the dinner bell," I said and gave him one last rub.

A little moan escaped his lips, quickly hidden by a mouthful of whatever the waiter had set in front of him. He gave out a longer, louder moan and looked down in surprise at his food. "Wow."

"That good?"

"Yes." He nodded for emphasis.

"What is it?"

"Osso buco with Risotto."

"Gesundheit."

"That wasn't a sneeze."

"You sure? Kinda sounded like a sneeze."

"No. It's Italian. Braised veal. Want a bite?"

"You really expect me to eat baby cow, you murderer?"

"I didn't cook it. I'm just eating it."

"I'm just teasing. Yes, I want a fucking bite."

He scooped out some of the fall-off-the-bone meat and paired it with a tiny bite of the big fluffy rice and held it out for me. I leaned over and let his fork slide into my mouth, wiggling my eyebrows at him as I did.

"Woah."

"See?"

"I'm still mad at you, though."

"What? Why? What did I do?"

"You moaned louder when you took a bite of that than when I was rubbing your junk. That's a fox paws."

"Fox paws?"

"Faux pas."

He shook his head and offered me another bite in apology. Not one to refuse food, or a properly prepared bribe and apology, I took it, moaning even louder than he did.

"You better be moaning pretty damn loud, later."

"Assuming you're getting some."

"Kaede..." His eyes scrunched in worry.

"Shush. I'm teasing. Finish your food."

He sighed, something was bothering him, and I had no idea what it was, but we were on a date and having fun. Mood killers could come later. So, could he.

My food on the other hand, while it looked delicious, was a complete and utter mystery to me. Just like Remy's plate, mine was true to my heritage and looked Japanese in nature, but that didn't exactly give me a clue. There were literally thousands of traditional Japanese dishes and while it was beautifully prepared, I was at a loss. Taking the silver chopsticks, I picked up a bit of it and popped it into my mouth. "OMFK"

"Oh em eff kay?"

"Oh, my friggin *kami*. This is Okonomiyaki."

"Bless you."

"Shut up. That doesn't sound anything like a sneeze. Try this."

I sliced a piece of the thick pancake layered with cabbage, vegetables, and seafood with my chopsticks and held it out for him. He looked at it dubiously, but gave in and took it daintily. He chewed for a moment, and then all the flavors bombarded his tongue like a cluster of fireworks. His eyes widened, and he smiled. "We're going to have to come back to this restaurant."

"Hell to the friggin yeah, we are. Think they would adopt me? This place has two floors, maybe they have a spare bedroom above. I could wash dishes."

We ate in silence and drank, not to get drunk, but to compliment the meal we were plowing through. Remy finished first, but I was picking at the last few bites, not because I was full, but because I didn't want the meal to end. It was the best time I'd had since coming to Iceland. The meal was fantastic, but the company was perfect. Every time he flashed me a smile, I got a little warmer inside.

"That was amazing," Remy said, breaking the silence.

"Fuck yes, it was." I practically lay back in the chair, rubbing my happy belly. Remy's eyes were following the movements of my hands. It was time for a little pre-dessert teasing.

Letting them slide down over my skirt, I "accidentally" let it rise up as I moved them back over my tummy. He stopped following my hands and focused intently on the front of my panties. If there had been anybody else in the restaurant, they would have gotten *quite* the show, too.

"Kaede."

"You like?"

He nodded, unable to tear his eyes away.

The door chimed, and I quickly flipped my skirt down, covering myself before anybody saw me. When Roki, David, and Rome walked in, I was kind of sorry I had. Raising my hand into the air, I waved at them to get their attention. Roki saw me first. Of course. I was pretty sure he had hidden a GPS tracker on me somewhere. The man could find me in a crowded bar thirteen blocks away. He always said he just followed his nose, but I'm pretty sure he used tracking software.

"Kaede-*sama*," he said with a relieved grin as he walked up to the table. "Rome-*sama*," he gave him a little bow.

"Ha! Your nose is off tonight. This is Remy."

"Kaede…"

I turned and grinned at Rome, until I saw the worried look on his face. "Remy?"

He shook his head.

My heart stopped. The conversation we'd had about him, me touching his junk, the kisses…the great conversation, the romantic dinner, the snuggles… All of it came flooding back, and I narrowed my eyes.

"Rome." I made his name a sneer of recognition.

His eyebrows shot up into his hairline, and he held out his hands to try and calm me down before I flipped serious shit on his lying ass. "Kaede, I've been *trying*–"

His words were interrupted with my fist. Even I was surprised I punched him in the mouth, and all I could do was stare at my hand. The skin on my middle knuckle split open, and I was bleeding. I must have cut it on his tooth. Looking up, I took solace in the fact that his lip looked worse than my knuckle. His eyes were closed, but it didn't look like it was from the pain I'd caused him, more like the pain he had caused me.

"Fuck you, Rome. Why the fuck did you lie to me?"

He sat silently as I stood up and pushed through the three of them standing there, not stopping until I was out the front door of the restaurant. I hadn't even gotten a chance to say goodbye to our wonderful hosts or thank them for the wonderful meal. The meal that would forever haunt my memory of an almost perfect date with the biggest asshole on the planet.

Chapter 10

I could hear their shouts behind me, and it tore my heart to ignore them. I just wanted to be alone for several years, until I got over the embarrassment factor of being tricked.

"At least I didn't jump him."

Maybe you should have. Guilt would be a wonderful punishment.

The *last* thing I needed was a Fenrir shaped earworm in my head. *He'd probably smile and tell his buddies.*

I do not think so. He seems to care for you a great deal.

Friends don't trick friends into showing them their panties.

Did he ask you to?

Look, you've been out of the dating game for a couple thousand years, I don't think you're exactly qualified to be having this discussion.

I felt him leave my consciousness with a small, *Humph.* I put a tic mark in my win column. The score was like fifty-eight thousand to three, but I always rooted for the underdog. Especially when it was me.

The voices were getting closer, yelling my name as loud as they could. Tears freezing in the wind, I popped to the end of the intersection, turned the corner, and popped another block away. Ignoring the looks the people of Oddi were giving me, I covered my face and ran as fast as I could, peeking through my fingers and looking for a cab.

Then I realized how screwed I was. I didn't have fare for a charon cab, or a human cab.

I dropped to the icy ground beneath me and drew my knees up to my chest, burying my face in my knees and giving up. They would find me sooner or later. I just hoped my ass didn't freeze to the concrete before then. None of them had a spatula.

Two sets of hands pulled me from the ground and straightened my skirt over my exposed butt. I assumed it was Roki and David, but the smell was wrong, spicier and less familiar. Looking up, I gasped as Kottr and Fress gave me an apologetic look.

"You wish to be away from the ones chasing you?"

"Yes," I managed to get out between sobs.

"Get on," Kottr said with his deep voice.

"Get on what?"

He and Fress left me standing there, walking away from me and melting into two giant felines. A golden chariot appeared out of nowhere and hitched itself to harnesses around their chest. They both looked over their shoulders with feline eyes, one gold and one blue in each head and nodded to the chariot behind them.

My name spurred me into action, and I leapt on, grabbing the reins in the holder. Without a word they took off and time stopped as we raced through the still roads of Oddi and into the fields of snow on the outskirts of the village.

I didn't have to direct them, and I had no need to ask where we were heading. I knew the way back to the Academy, and we didn't stop until we rolled up to the gates leading to the school.

My hands were frozen, and I had difficulty letting go of the leather strap between them. Fress was at my side in a moment, gently uncurling my hands and rubbing them between his hands. When they still wouldn't uncurl, he brought them to his lips and breathed his warm breath over them, gently massaging them.

"Thank you," I managed to whisper between chattering teeth.

"You are welcome. I am sorry you are unused to our weather."

"It gets cold in California, but *nothing* like this."

"Come, let us get you into the school and warm."

"I can manage. Thank you," I stammered and stepped off the sloped floor of the chariot.

"The goddess would never forgive us if anything happened to you. Come. We will tend you."

I turned around and the Chariot and Kitty Kottr was gone, he was standing there again in his human form. "Kottr and Fress. The cats who pull the chariot of the goddess Freya in battle. I knew I'd heard your names before."

They both grinned at me, each taking an arm and helping me up the steps, not carrying me, but I'd almost wish they had. I couldn't move. The cold had seeped into my bones, and my muscles were cramping. My leg locked up and Fress scooped me into his arms.

"Shift."

"C-c-can't. Some-o-one will-l see."

He frowned. "The contest."

I nodded.

He just shook his head and flashed an angry stare at the main building, like it was the buildings fault. Maybe he was giving a mental finger to Uncle Tatsuo. It was sweet either way.

"I'll be okay. You're warm."

He nodded and picked up the pace, heading for our dormitory building. "Kottr…" The rest of whatever he said was lost to me as it was in Old Norse.

Kottr nodded at him once and ran ahead.

"Where's he going?"

"To prepare a hot bath for you."

"Pretty sure I'm going to be stuck with a lukewarm shower, but I appreciate the thought."

He smirked and picked up the pace, moving as swiftly through the school entrance as he could. With the added weight of me, he was no match for the speed of his partner, but we were still moving fast enough for the wind to whistle in my ear. It wasn't helping my temperature situation at all, so I buried my face into his chest and closed my eyes.

"Stay awake, Kaede."

"C-c-can't."

"Yes, you can. We are almost there."

"Where?"

"Our room."

"But I live with Roki."

"Not your room, my room."

"You're taking me to your room? Is there a bed? What about food?" I wasn't even sure if he could understand my incoherent mumblings.

"Food, bed, and bath."

"And beyond?"

"Beyond what?"

"Infinity."

"What are you talking about?"

"Not what, where. We need to go there."

"Where?"

"To infinity. And Bed, Bath, and Beyond."

I couldn't hear his laugh, but I felt it when my eyebrows started rubbing up and down his chest. Then the laughter turned into something else. A rumbling purr started in his chest, lulling my senses.

"If you want me to stay awake, you better stop putting me to sleep."

"How am I putting you to sleep?"

"Stop purring, kitty."

"My apologies."

"Don't. 'Twas nice."

He lowered me, reaching out and opening one of the double doors leading into Breckenridge Hall, and deftly swung me inside, avoiding banging my head or feet against the frame. "We are home."

"Home is where you hang your head."

"The bath is ready," Kottr's voice said worriedly from the stairs.

"Good. She is delirious."

"Come, brother. Let us warm her."

"Brother?" I blinked up in surprise at Fress. "Got the whole 'you two are a couple' vibe from you. I didn't know you were brothers."

"Brothers in duty and form. We are not related. He uses brother as a term of endearment."

"So. You are?"

"What?"

"A couple?" He jostled me, stepping up the stairs and heading for our floor.

"You mean together? In a loving relationship?"

"Or a lusty one. Just curious."

"Yes."

"Oh. Called it!" I raised my hand in triumph. "Roki owes me twenty bucks."

"For?"

"We had a bet that you were gay. He swore up and down that the two of you were checking out my ass."

"We were. Your tails, more specifically."

"They weren't out at the club!"

We made it to the top of the landing, and Kottr held the door open for us. "No, but they are still visible to those who know how to look."

"You can see my tails?"

"*Ja.*"

I blushed. My tails weren't something I normally let people see on purpose. I even had trouble letting Roki groom them. Now Fress was telling me he couldn't *not* see them. It felt like accidentally flashing someone a titty. "Well, don't stare at them."

"I shall not." He scrunched his face and smiled at me. It was the most un-catlike gesture I'd ever seen from him.

Kottr held the door to their room open, and Fress maneuvered me through and into their room. A room that looked *nothing* like the typical dorm rooms at Aesir Academy…

They had one queen-sized canopy bed, a single dresser, and a larger desk than the single ones in our room. The solitary versions of furniture left most of the room open, even with the queen bed. That space was currently occupied by a copper tub filled with steaming water. I practically groaned when I saw it.

"How?"

"Magic," Fress answered with a little chuckle, setting me on my feet. He pulled my blazer off, tossed it on the bed, and immediately got to work on my buttons. I slapped his hand.

"I am perfectly capable of taking off my own damn clothes. Just as you are perfectly capable of turning around. I don't care if you are gay."

He chuckled softly and did as I asked. I was sliding my panties down when I noticed Kottr standing by the door, watching me intently.

"Uh…"

"My apologies," he said and turned. "I assumed you were talking to Fress."

"Uh huh." I finished undressing and stepped over the side of the copper tub and winced as the overly warm water lapped at my toes. "Hot, hot, hot."

"You like it?"

"I like it. Hot, hot, hot," I sang as I plunged my leg up to my knee. The other followed, and I had to dip my ass in the water four times until I could finally submerge myself up to my neck. The only problem was the water was crystal clear and wasn't going to hide a damn thing. "Fuck it."

"Are you in?"

"Yes."

Fress turned around, and Kottr perched on the end of the bed as warmth *finally* crept its way into my frozen bones. "Better?"

"You have no idea," I said happily. "So, you just keep a tub in your bedroom? This isn't something you just magicked up for my benefit?"

"We are...very clean conscious. Showers do not substitute for a good soak in a tub."

"You're sure you two aren't Japanese?"

"Quite." Kottr answered, sounding almost miffed.

Fress was rummaging around behind me, and I didn't think anything of it until a bowl dipped into the water in front of me. "Lean forward for a moment."

"Uh...why?"

"Do you not wish for your hair to be washed?"

Okay, in my defense, the entire situation, while surreal, didn't have a single solitary sexual feeling to it whatsoever. So, I found myself leaning forward in the tub and hugging my knees before I knew it. There were few things I loved in the world half as much as someone washing my hair. When he gently poured the water over my hair, I practically cooed.

"You have beautiful hair."

"Thanks, Fressy."

"Fressy?"

"Yerp." I immediately regretted my regression to ermagerdian. He probably wasn't ready for that level of Kaede. Luckily, he ignored it.

"Fressy," Kottr said and chuckled throatily.

"You may shush. Why don't you get our guest some tea?"

He nodded, got up, and surprisingly left the room. "Is he going to go all the way to the dining hall for some tea?"

Fress leaned over putting his lips next to my ear. "Mostly to smoke his cigarettes. I hate them and won't allow him to smoke in our room, so I send him on little errands."

I nodded appreciatively. "That's kind of brilliant. I should try that with Hiroki."

"Your friend smokes?"

"No, but he likes to complain about my life choices. Little hard to do if he's fetching me ice cream."

"Are you two mated?"

"We mate, but not like you mean. He's one of my boyfriends and we bork."

"Bork?"

"Bang, shimmy, shine. Polish, boink, bow chicky wow-wow."

"Make love?"

"Every time."

"You love him."

"With everything I am."

"Does that leave room for the others?"

"I gotta lotta love to give."

He had started massaging the clove-smelling shampoo into my hair, and I leaned back, letting my wet hair hang over the side of the tub and enjoying the feeling of my brain melting.

"Do they get jealous?"

"My boys? Hell no. They don't have a jealous bone in their body."

There was a loud crash as the door to the bedroom was kicked open. The wood splintered into the bedroom, and the boys in question poured into the room like a SWAT team after a fresh box of Krispy Kremes.

One of the twins launched himself, transformed, and landed atop Fress, clamping his neck tightly in his jaws. Roki had his sword drawn, but let go of it as he stared at me sitting naked in a tub full of sudsy water. It disappeared before it hit the ground. David just stood by the door, hands over his mouth in shock as the other twin frantically looked around the room for Kottr.

I looked over my shoulder at Fress as he stared at me, practically begging me to get the giant hellhound off his neck. "Well, maybe sometimes," I said apologetically and shrugged. "Romy, you wanna let go of my friend?"

He let go of him with a slight *ptui* noise and a *thud* as Fress' head hit the floor with a wet sound I hoped wasn't doggy drool.

A tea set made another loud crash as Kottr walked into the room and surveyed the damage. "What happened?" His voice rumbled in shock, not anger.

"Welcome back, Kottr." I stared at him as I realized what I said, remembering the reruns of the Seventies sitcom Roki had forced me to watch when he realized John Travolta was in it, and I burst out laughing. Water splashed on the floor as I slapped my knee. "Welcome back, Mista Kotta!"

Chapter 11

Prostrated on the floor, forehead pressed to his fingertips, Roki was begging for my forgiveness. "Kaede-*sama*, I am truly sorry."

"For?"

"Rushing to conclusions."

"And?"

He sighed and lifted his head from the floor, giving me a truly pathetic look. "And for not believing you when you said that nothing happened between you and the Icelanders. Even though you were naked in a tub of water, and he was massaging you."

"Shampooing."

"*Hai*. That."

Sighing, I motioned for him to get up. I was all for teasing Roki, but when he prostrated himself like that, it made me feel a little uncomfortable. I couldn't have blamed him for jumping to conclusions, either. If he had been in the tub with Fress shampooing his hair, I would have grabbed a camera and stayed to watch the show. And then I would have smacked the crap out of him for cheating on me. Us. I meant us. "I forgive you."

He rolled his eyes as he stood. Hiroki was learning. "Why did you run off?"

His question brought a brief but fierce snarl to my lips. "Ask Romeo."

"Rome-*sama*?"

"Rome-*baka*." I changed the honorific to idiot. It fit him a little more.

"Did he hurt you?"

"No. He made a fool out of me." I dropped my ass on Roki's bed and pouted.

"He assisted your natural ability, or was solely responsible?" Roki snickered at his joke.

"This was all on him. I are innocents."

Roki cocked an eyebrow, doubt still evident on his face. "What did he do?"

"He was sweet, attentive, caring…almost the perfect date. I was having a great time!"

"That bastard. Should I implement plan 18-A?"

"That's the one with the tarantulas?"

"No. That is 18-C. A involves peppering his underpants with Lyme infested ticks."

"Ouch. Go with the tarantulas."

"Because he was the ideal date? Maybe I should just take his head."

"Roki…he told me he was Remy."

Understanding finally brightened his features. "Oh."

He sat down on the bed next to me, and I leaned against him, putting my head on his shoulder. "Why? For weeks he's insisted that he gets upset when I mistake him for his brother, and now, he wants to pretend to be him? I don't get it."

Roki sighed, and my head bobbed against his shoulder. "I am sorry, Kaede-*sama*."

"You apologize enough for yourself. Don't apologize for the stupidity of others."

"You misunderstand. I am not apologizing for his actions. I'm apologizing for interrupting your date."

"What? Why?"

"Because you were enjoying yourself, and we did not see how it would end."

"With my foot impacting his testicles with enough force to permanently change the timbre of his voice by at least three octaves?"

"No. For him to tell you the truth."

"You think he would have?"

"I have little doubt."

"Before or after we had sex?"

He turned and put me at arm's length, holding my shoulders gently. "If you have such little faith in Rome, perhaps you should not date him again in the future."

Shaking my head, I held up my hands. "No. I don't think he would have."

"Neither do I. He knows what would have happened to his reproductive organs if he had."

"My foot?"

Roki shook his head. "My sword."

"Big head or little head?"

"Most likely both."

I couldn't stand it anymore. I got all frisky and wet when he got all growly and protective like that. It was one of the reasons I fell in love with him so, so long ago. He let go of my shoulders as I pushed forward and wrapped my arms around him, falling over him and snuggling into his side. He lifted his head from the bed, and I met his lips with mine. His tongue had just slipped against mine when a knock at the door interrupted us.

"Really?" I looked over at the door and debated ignoring whoever it was. Unfortunately, all my boyfriends were of the canine variety and could probably hear me breathing from twenty feet away, even through the door. "Coming," I said testily.

"Want me to answer it?" Roki was sitting up, but I shook his head as I crawled off him, giving his Roki-bits a gentle squeeze as I did.

"No. It might be Rome. His balls have a date with my toes." Practically stomping to the door, I flung it open to a very contrite looking David standing there. "'Snot Rome. It's a David," I said to Roki and stepped aside, letting David in.

He didn't walk past me, stopping just inside the door and closing it behind him and pulling me into his arms. "Are you okay?"

"Yeah. Why?"

"Just came from across the hall. Rome told Remy and I what he did."

Pulling back, I held up my hand in front of David's face. "I don't want to hear whatever excuse he gave you. If he wants to apologize, he's going to be sucking my butt for the next decade."

"You mean kissing?"

"This is beyond kissing. He can French kiss my ass for forgiveness."

David stared at me. "You want him to use tongue…"

And then I realized what I'd said and turned crimson. My head probably could have guided Santa's sleigh one foggy Christmas Eve. "That is *not* what I meant!"

Roki's snickers echoed from the other room.

"I meant this goes beyond kissing my ass… He fucked up royally, and it will be a hot day in Valhalla before I forgive his lying, deceitful ass."

"Okay, then. I won't get involved."

I lifted myself up on my tiptoes and brushed my lips against his. "Smart boy."

Grabbing his hand, I pulled him the rest of the way into our room and motioned to my bed. "Have a seat."

"You guys want to go watch a movie or something? It's too early to call it a night."

"I wish we had some cards or something." I sat back down next to Roki and crisscrossed my legs. "Don't really feel like being around a bunch of people."

Roki slid his hand up my back and comfortingly rubbed the spot between my shoulder blades.

"That feels good." I smiled over at him and then turned my head toward David. He was sitting on the bed, feet on the floor, and leaning back, his hands supporting him. His eyes were focused two feet below my eyes.

When I'd sat down on the bed in my skirt and crisscrossed my legs, I'd inadvertently exposed my panties to him. He was in seventh heaven, practically drooling over the white cotton. His favorite. Roki gave me a quizzical look as I leaned back on one of my elbows and straightened one leg. I just gave him a casual wink and let my eyes flick in David's direction. He glanced at David and gave a small smirk.

"So, what happened after I stormed out of the restaurant?" I figured small talk would be a good way to let David enjoy his show. Me, being the little tease that I am, reached down and absentmindedly scratched my thigh, hiking up my skirt without looking. Not over my underwear, but high enough to give David something to *really* look at. I swear I heard him moan a little.

"We chased after you," Roki said.

"And then what?"

"Followed you to the newcomers' room."

"What did you do after that?" I gave him a dirty look. I probably should have picked someone better to engage in small talk with. Like a mime.

"I felt my heart cleft in twain at the sight of you, as bare as the day you were born, in a tub in the room of two men. One of whom, I might add, had difficulty keeping his hands from your flesh as the other waited on you."

127

Okay. Let's not overdo it. "Thankfully, they got me in that tub to warm me up."

"*Hai.*"

I lifted my leg and put my foot on the bed, bending my knee and shifting my leg from side to side. His view had to have been perfect, and the movement of my leg was spreading my lips beneath the soft fabric. I could feel the moisture practically dripping from me at the thought of David drooling from his seat across from me. Unable to stand it anymore, I looked up at him.

As I suspected, his mouth was open, and his eyes were glued to me. He had even unconsciously leaned forward to get a better view, and if I wasn't mistaken, there was a slight throbbing movement in his pants.

"Whatcha looking at David?"

He finally tore his eyes away and looked up at me hopelessly. "Uhhh."

So articulate. "Are you looking at my *panties*, David?"

He nodded slightly, color brightening his cheeks. "I'm sorry."

"It's okay. I don't mind if it's you…" I made my voice as meek as possible, lowering my eyes, and blinking at him. "Do you like looking there?"

"You know I do." He blew out the breath of air he'd been holding.

"What if I were to do this?" I slipped my finger behind the front of my panties and squeezing the fabric together, exposing a bit of my hair and the sides of my pussy to him, but hiding my sopping wetness.

His eyes bulged in his head, and he started breathing a little heavier. "Yes."

"Yes? Yes, you want me to cover back up, or yes, you like it?"

"Like."

128

He was starting to sound like Roki. I looked over at him and he was staring just as hard as David, but his view wasn't nearly as good. "What about you, Roki? Do you want to go sit by David? You'll have a better view."

He didn't need to be asked twice. Getting up, he crossed the space between our bed with one long step, turned, and plopped down next to David. I reached up to the head of the bed, grabbed a couple of pillows, and tucked them beneath my head. I lay back but could still see the two of them. Putting my other foot down on the bed, I spread my legs and lifted my skirt up over my stomach, all pretenses of innocence chucked out the window like a bag of weed with the cops knocking on the door.

Gripping my panties in my fingers, I pulled it tight into my valley, my lips engulfing the gusset, and my clit making a hard lump against the white fabric. Reaching down with my other hand, I slipped my index finger into my almost exposed wetness and then rubbed it in little circles over my clit as they watched.

"Oooh. That feels good," I said almost shrilly, not lying as pleasure swept through me.

"She smells amazing."

"*Hai.*"

They both looked at each other and smiled before turning back. I needed more. Pulling my panties to the side, I slipped a finger inside me, bucking my hips and then letting the finger glide back out, spreading my wetness all over my clit as my motions became a little faster. Almost frantic.

"Touch yourselves," I said almost breathlessly, wanting to see them do just that.

David didn't hesitate, standing and pushing his pants and underwear, if he was wearing any, down to his knees and sitting back down. Leaning back on one hand, he began stroking his cock with the other.

Poor Roki didn't know where to look. Finally, he stood and did the same, eyes settling back down on my spread pussy. I felt like I won a small victory.

"Oooooh, " I cooed and added another finger, letting my clit dance between them.

"Take your panties off, Kaede-*sama*."

"No. Leave them on, please," David practically begged.

I compromised and slid them down just a bit, letting them drape over me loosely as I let my fingers slip back inside me.

"Fuck that's hot." David was stroking himself in time to the movements of my fingers.

"Wouldn't it feel better if somebody else were doing that?" I let my eyes drift between the two of them, letting them know I was speaking to both.

They looked at each other, and their hands let go of themselves, crossed, and touched each other. "She was right," David said with a chuckle and a hiss as Roki stroked him faster.

Roki just nodded.

I almost came. Every time I think they can't do anything hotter than what we've already done, they surprise me. Most of the time it wasn't them going farther, but doing something simple like stroking each other that *really* floated my goat.

It was like they shared a mental connection. Standing at the same time, they walked over to me, still stroking each other as I fingered myself inches from them. "Do you want us to come on you? Or do you want us to fuck you?"

David's forthright question caused me to gush a little. I liked it when he talked dirty, I just hadn't known he could. I stopped masturbating and begged them to slip themselves inside me with my eyes, I didn't care where.

They let go of each other's cocks and nodded at each other, another unspoken agreement between them. For all I knew, they had made plans in case an opportunity such as this arose. Roki sat down next to me and motioned for me to stand. Curious, I did as he asked. He pulled me between his legs, and bent down a little, letting his tongue slide up between my lips before he kissed my tummy, just above my pubic hair. "She tastes even better than she smells."

Roki turned me around, and David leaned in for a kiss. It wasn't gentle, either. He practically devoured me with his mouth as I groaned against him. Roki's fingers slipped up inside me from behind, and I parted my legs. He began pumping them in and out of me, David refusing to let go of my lips as I tried to gasp through the pleasure. The orgasm caught me off guard, I had completely missed the telltale signs of its approach, and David released me as I tossed my head back and let out cry of pleasure.

Roki's fingers slowed as I started to come down, and David looked at me embarrassedly. "That was uh…pretty loud."

"Sorry," I mumbled, having difficulty forming words. And thoughts.

"Don't be. That was hot."

I looked over his shoulder. "Think they heard?"

"So did the students at the other end of the school, most likely."

I chuckled until Roki's hands gripped my hips and pulled me down into his lap. I felt his cock pressing up against me as his hands slid up under my shirt and grabbed my breasts as his lips found my neck. His breath sent shivers over my skin as he kissed down along my flesh to my shoulder.

David unbuttoned my shirt, getting down on his knees to get the lower buttons, and then letting his fingers trail through my tuft of white just below the hem of my shirt.

131

He parted my thighs, draping them over Roki's. I settled in his lap a little further and leaned back against him.

Roki's lips trailed down over my shoulder now that my shirt was open, and he let his teeth slide over my skin as his hands slid down my stomach and over my pussy, pulling my lips apart.

David reached down between my legs and took ahold of Roki's cock. Roki lifted me for a moment, and David guided the tip of Roki's cock to my wet hole. When Roki let go of me, I cried out as his hardness parted me, slipping inside me as David leaned over and sucked my clit into his mouth.

"Holy fuck fuck fuck." I involuntarily started bouncing on Roki.

The angle was awkward, and Roki slipped out of me. David looked up and smiled at me before gripping Roki and sucking my juices off him. From my perspective, it looked like David was sucking my cock, and I shuddered at the hotness of the situation.

When David guided Roki back into me, he stood and offered me his cock. I never wanted anything more as I gripped him in my hand and pulled him to my mouth. A cock in my pussy and one in my mouth was not how I thought the day was going to end, I was just grateful it had.

David stroked my cheek lovingly with one hand as he smiled down at me. Grinning around a mouthful of his cock, I winked at him as his breathing quickened. He was close, damn close. I pulled him from my mouth with a squelched *pop*. "You gonna cum?"

He nodded.

I let go of him and reached around, grabbing a handful of ass with each hand to pull him closer. Parting my lips, I let them glide over his tip as I slowly pulled him in my mouth using every ounce of suction I could muster. Slowly working down his length, I had three-quarters of him in my mouth, his tip practically touching the back of my throat as he started grunting, and I felt the first splash against the very back of my tongue.

His fingers combed through my hair, grabbing two handfuls as he gently bucked his hips against me, my nose bumping against him as he came. I held him there as he finished and for a few moments after, letting my tongue graze his flesh as aftershocks of pleasure caused him to make cute noises. When he called my name shakily, I let him go and licked my lips.

He sat down on the bed across from us and then got down on the floor, crawling toward me as Roki fucked me.

"Come for me, Kaede," Roki whispered in my ear. He slid his hands back up to my breasts, trapping my nipples between his fingers and squeezing gently.

I hissed and began to grind my hips against him, focusing on the pleasure spreading from where his flesh touched the deepest places inside me. He started bucking me in his lap, and the pleasure spilled through me. I began calling his name in time with his thrusts, building up volume as the intensity of my orgasm began to build.

David kissed the juncture of my opening where Roki's cock entered me. I reached down and grabbed his head, pulling him closer. He licked from that spot, letting the cock driving into me slip against his tongue and then sweeping it over my pussy until the tip of it settled on my clit and began gently lapping, just as I couldn't hold back my orgasm for another moment.

I came, throwing myself back against Roki's solid chest and squeezing David's head between my thighs.

"David!" Roki hissed his name, knowing I was useless.

David's fingers slid across my opening as he forcibly removed Roki's cock and pumping it with his hand. I opened my legs and looked down, just as Roki erupted over my stomach, his hot seed slowly sliding down my skin.

David licked my flesh wherever it splashed.

"That's fucking hotter," I mumbled, remembering David's statement from before.

David smiled and planted one last kiss on my still sensitive clit. I shuddered as he stood and offered me his hand.

Standing, I threw my arms around him, burying my face in his chest.

"Better than cards?"

"Like crazy eights, but I've played some seriously fun games of Uno."

"You're a shit."

"Yep."

I smiled as he laughed.

"David?"

"Yes, Kaede?"

"Would you sleep with us tonight?"

I looked back at Hiroki to make sure it was okay with him. He grinned and nodded, still out of breath.

"You want me to sleep with you or Hiroki?" He sounded a little skeptical.

"Both of us. Let's push the bed together."

"I'd like that."

"I get to be in the middle." I looked back at Roki and stuck my tongue out at him.

"Of course, Kaede-*sama*. The monkey is *always* in the middle."

Chapter 12

Staring in shock, I watched as the doctor disappeared through the door and closed it behind him. My mouth was still hanging open as I turned and looked at Lornca. She'd been a welcome presence, for once, through the entire examination. I was in shock because I hadn't even had to get naked.

"That was it?" He had literally waved his green glowing hands over my abdomen, nodded once to Lornca without a word, and left the room.

"If you are dissatisfied, I could find some metal objects to probe you with."

"Uh, no. Insert that whole phrase about gift horses and mouths here."

She smiled and walked over to one of the cabinets in the examination room, opening it and pulling out a sealed, sterile med kit.

Oh. Here comes the bad part. "What's it going to be? Pills? Patch? Injection? Insertion of some sort of IUD?"

She narrowed her eyes and ripped open the package. I gulped audibly. "Give me your wrist."

Nearly shaking, I held it out for her. She reached into the sterile package and pulled out what looked like a beaded bracelet, onyx gleaming brightly under the fluorescent lighting above.

"Where does that go?" Sweat started to bead on my forehead.

She slipped it over my hand, letting it snap against my wrist. "There you go. Now you can't get pregnant as long as you wear that."

"Seriously?"

"Seriously."

"What? Does it release hormones directly into my bloodstream?"

"Nope. It is magic that keeps you from ovulating."

"Shut up."

She pulled back and gave me a stern look.

"I don't mean that literally. It's like get out. Or no way."

"I know. I am just screwing with you. I'm an elf, not a square."

"Uh… Sure."

"You're all set. Come back if you experience any side effects."

"Like nausea, vomiting, diarrhea, uncontrollable flatulence, aches, pains, or death?"

"No. More like an increase of breast volume, or hair growing where it shouldn't."

I stared at her. "I'm not that lucky. As for the hair…" I shifted into my demi form. "Not too worried about that."

"So, I see. Your form hasn't changed anymore since the last time you were here. That's promising."

"Let's hope it stays that way." I nodded for emphasis. "So, how long does it take for this thing to start working?"

She glanced down at the watch on her wrist and back up to me. "About three minutes ago."

"Really?"

"Really," she said with a chuckle and motioned me toward the door. "Have fun." She gave me a long, slow, drawn out wink.

I blushed horribly and slipped out the door, not daring to look back, and headed for the Dining Hall. My appointment had been for just before lunch, and I'd been too nervous to eat. My stomach was threatening to stage a revolt, and it felt like a land war had already erupted.

"Kaede?"

I stopped in my tracks, turning slowly and giving a little gasp as my father stood there looking from me to the door of the infirmary. "Father?"

"Are you…all right?"

Nodding nervously, a billion-and-a-half excuses as to why I was in the infirmary prioritized themselves through my brain. "*Hai.*" I was going with the classic, 'Don't volunteer any information, keep it simple, and only speak when spoken to' ploy. It was usually the safest bet when dealing with the Father. He saw through lies better than most mothers.

"That is good. No lasting effects from the attacks?"

"No."

"What were you doing in the infirmary then?"

I'd been half convinced he wasn't going to ask. My face contorted in fear when he finally did. He must have realized, and his eyes widened as he held up his hands.

"Forget I asked!" Then he shook his head and turned around.

"Papa?"

He halted that first step away and turned back, slowly. "*Hai?*"

"It was for female things. Everything is okay. Would you care to have lunch?"

I swear to fuck, the man smiled. "*Hai.*"

Sliding my arm through his, I pressed my face against his arm in a very uncharacteristic motion of affection and let him lead the way to the Dining Hall. The boys were on their own. They could live without me for one meal. I hoped.

"Are you sure you are okay? This is very unlike you." He motioned to my arms wrapped around his.

"I know. Just the way things have been going lately… Papa, I'm tired of fighting."

He didn't sigh, it was like every breath he had ever held in the past twenty-years or so of my existence finally escaped from him in relief. I could feel the tension and anger leaving him, all from my simple act of kindness. Maybe he could tell I meant what I said.

"Papa?"

"Yes, Kaede?"

"I'm sorry."

"What for?"

"Everything." I hugged his arm a little tighter, concentrating on not getting my feet tangled with his as we walked.

He stopped our journey through the halls of Aesir Academy, pulled his arm from mine, held me out at arm's length, and bent down to look into my eyes. "As am I, Daughter." Then he hugged me, and I can neither confirm nor deny, but both of us might have been crying a little, maybe.

"She is mine." Fenrir ruined the moment, his resonant voice echoing from my vocal cords as my father and I *finally* shared a brief moment of reconciliation.

I expected my father to push me away to argue with the mythic wolf, but he didn't. He refused to let me go and just whispered, "No. She belongs to no one but herself."

My misty eyes turned into full sobs as my father held me tight. "Thank you, Papa."

"Fight him, Kaede," he said and finally released me. "Still hungry?"

"Famished."

138

It was the first peaceful meal I had shared with my father in over a decade. As we sat at the table, smiling and laughing, Hiroki beamed at me from across the dining room. His happiness was almost greater than mine.

Remy and David seemed happy, too. Rome was brooding and looking worried as I flipped him off whenever my father was looking at his food.

∞ ∞ ∞

"Kaede."

I had just said goodbye to my father. He was flying home in the morning but promised to be back in a week. He also had a plan to help rid me of Fenrir, but he wouldn't elaborate, tapping his ear to let me know he didn't want the wolf god to hear. After all that, Rome's voice behind me was the last thing in the universe I wanted to hear, but there we were. There wasn't a doubt that it was him either.

"What?" I didn't bother turning around.

"Can we talk?"

"No." I started walking away, heading back to our dormitory where I could put two-and-a-half inches of solid, locking wood between us.

"Please?"

My foot froze, rooted in place. I think it was the please that did it. Sighing, I turned around. "Talk?"

"Yes. Just talk."

I walked past him and headed back into the dining hall. If he wanted to talk, I was going to need coffee to stay awake. I had absolutely no desire to hear whatever lie he had concocted to excuse his behavior, but I would at least hear him out before I disemboweled him with a spork.

"Where are you going?"

"Coffee," I said in answer.

"I was hoping we could talk somewhere private."

"We'll get a table in the corner. Trust me. You don't want to be alone in the same room as me right now, Rome."

"Fair enough."

I was passing the dessert section when my hand shot out of its own volition and snagged a plate with a largish slice of cheesecake topped with strawberries on it. Almost putting it back, I realized it might make the situation a little less volatile. I couldn't chew Rome's ankles off with cheeks stuffed full of cheesecake. So, I carried it over to the beverage bar, poured myself a cup of coffee, and headed for a secluded little table for two in the back corner. There would be less witnesses if the cheesecake failed to keep me from gutting him.

Just as I was about to pull the mug from under the spigot, Rome's hand intercepted the cup, almost sloshing its contents in order to grab it. "You have your hands full. I'll carry it."

I walked away without so much as a word of thanks.

The Dining Hall was damn near deserted, and we had our pick of tables. True to my word, I chose one in the far back corner. I didn't want any complaints of a foul-mouthed student berating a classmate to make its way to the headmaster.

With both of his hands full, Rome couldn't pull out my chair, even though I could tell by the look on his face he really wanted to. I had one hand free, but I still kicked the chair away from the table and sat. It was always important to stretch before dishing out any degree of ass whooping. The last thing I wanted was to pull a hammy when I lodged my foot in Rome's rectum.

"Talk."

He set my coffee down in front of me and sat down as he sipped carefully from his cup. "I can't even begin to tell you how sorry I am."

140

"You better figure out a way."

"I know."

"You done fucked up, A-A-Ron."

"Pardon?"

"You fucked up! Do you have any *clue* as to how pissed I am at you right now? Why in the name of all that is holy would you pretend to be your fucking brother? Were you trying to score? Did you think pretending to be him would get you into my panties?" I paused to stuff a mound of cheesecake in my mouth, washing it down with a swallow of coffee, and not giving a shit that it felt like I had just poured molten lead into my pie hole. Cheesecake hole. Whatever. It burned, and I didn't care. "Of all the two-faced, moronic, self-centered, conniving, dirty, underhanded, bullshit things you could have, would have, or have done…that was the fucking worst." I swallowed, trying very hard to keep the cheesecake down. I must have swallowed wrong, and a piece of the ooey-gooey goodness lodged itself against one of the walls of my left ventricle. The heart that was beating a mile-a-minute felt like it was slowing and breaking. It hurt.

"I know I did. My intentions were good, but I fucked up by not telling you sooner. Even though I tried."

"Intentions were good? By tricking me into thinking you were someone you weren't. I don't know how I didn't see right away that you weren't Remy. *He* cares about me. Loves me. Would never hurt me."

"Neither would I."

"Braaaaaaa. Wrong answer. You already did. Probably worse than anyone ever has in my life up until that moment. I hate you, Rome. I fucking despise you. I hate that I was enjoying myself with you. I hate myself for being happy!" I slammed the fork sideways down into my cheesecake, ruining what was left of it and ignoring the fallout from my pastry attack. It had landed over both of us, but I was too busy sobbing to care.

"You were enjoying our date?"

"Was. Past tense. When I think about it now, I want to throw up."

"Kaede..."

"Don't. There is nothing in this *world* that could make me forgive you." Standing up, I started marching toward the door, mentally calling myself an idiot for even attempting to listen to him.

His arms kept me from getting more than three feet away.

"Let. Me. Go!" Slamming my head back against him, I was hoping to at least get a chin shot in. Unfortunately, our difference in height just meant he *might* have a bruise in two to three hours. His grip didn't loosen one bit.

"I'll let you go, but don't leave. Please, just let me tell you one thing."

His arms eased up on their hold and against my better judgement, I turned and stared at him. "What? I have a nail appointment to get to."

"I don't expect you to forgive me. I just wanted to tell you how sorry I was, and that I was an idiot. Things should never have gotten that far. My only intention was to put you at ease. I thought maybe if you thought I was Remy, you would. That was my only intention, I swear."

"Fine. Can I go now?"

Sighing, he nodded.

I turned around and started walking away slowly, fighting with every ounce of courage I had, not to run. When I was five feet away, I stopped and without turning around, asked him, "Would you have fucked me?"

"What?"

"You heard me. If things had progressed, would you have fucked me letting me think you were Remy?"

"The fact that your question makes me want to vomit, means my answer is a definite no. I wouldn't have."

"You probably should have. That might have been the only way you ever would have gotten a chance."

And I walked away.

Chapter 13

Surprisingly enough, smacking one's face against a linoleum covered countertop is a *damn* good way to sober the fuck up. Sitting up, I rubbed my nose and forehead, flashing a quick glance at Roki. His eyebrows were raised above his widened eyes, and a sympathetic look passed over his face. "Ouch."

"Didn't feel nuffin," I said and set my head back down, pressing my forehead against the cool countertop in an effort to alleviate any swelling. I'd been drinking since I stumbled back into our room the night before, woke up still drunk, and had been chewing on the hair of the dog since breakfast. It was the only thing that numbed the pain in my heart and the pounding in my head.

Even Professor Velheim had taken one look at me and decided to leave me alone. She had spent the better part of the class working with the students in the back. She was probably just ogling Kottr and Fress, but as long as it kept her off my ass, I didn't give a shit. Or even two.

"Kaede-*sama*, you look horrible."

"Gee. Thanks, Roki. Go suck a bag of dicks."

"Where exactly would one procure a bag of dicks?"

"I don't know. Dick's Sporting Goods? I'll get you a bag of dicks for your birthday," I mumbled and turned my head away from him, staring out the windows at the mountains in the distance.

"Please keep one of them for yourself."

"Don't need another dick."

"I meant to replace the one atop your shoulders."

"Huh?" I lifted my head and turned back toward him, staring incredulously. "Did you just call me a dick head?"

"If the prophylactic hat fits, wear it."

"Wait… Are you mad at me?"

He shrugged and stirred the pot. In more ways than one.

"What the fuck did I do?"

"Class is over in twenty minutes. We do not have time to discuss this."

"Woah. Hold on one *kami*-damned minute… You. Are pissed. At me? What fucking universe did I wake up in?" I looked around the room to make sure nobody had grown a second head or was at least growing a dick out of their forehead. I paused a brief moment to ponder the possibilities associated with *that*.

"It is nothing," Roki answered in his usual passive aggressive voice whenever I had finally dropped the final straw that broke the fox's back.

"Well, obviously it's fucking something. What did I do to you? Don't even start to tell me that you're pissed that I want to gut Rome."

He narrowed his eyes and shook his head. "No. As I said, it is nothing. Do not concern yourself."

"Fine." I reached under the sink and took a swig of my mead. "If you're not going to tell me, it just means you're a liar, liar, pants on fire." There was a subtle change in the air, and I stuck my finger in my ear and wiggled it around.

"Either way, it does not matter."

"Not to me."

"Good."

I felt bad whenever I was an ass to Roki. He was the last person on the planet that deserved it, and I knew that. I really did. But when he slipped into one of his rare moods, he was impossible to deal with. He'd be fine in a few hours once he vented his frustration on me. It was probably good for him. "Still love me?"

"Unfortunately."

"Ouch."

"Is the rice almost done?"

I glanced at the rice cooker in front of me. It was the one part of the meal that Roki had delegated to me. The display was blank, and I gasped when I realized I'd never turned it on. "Uh… Houston? We haz a problem."

"You forgot to turn it on, didn't you?"

"Maaaybe."

Blowing out an angry breath, he got up and pushed his stool back, heading for the walk-in cooler. "What do you need, Roki? I'll get it."

"No. You'd probably forget what you went in there for, and I'd have to come find you. It will be quicker to get it myself."

"Ouch."

He stopped walking and looked at me over his shoulder, cocking an eyebrow and flashing me a disgusted look. Chagrined, I pouted on my stool until he came back and slammed some zucchini down on the table next to me and pulled out a cutting board. I sat in silence, moderately drinking while I watched him deftly cut the squash up into thin noodle-like slices and slam them into the pan he had been reducing a sauce in, stirring it until they cooked. He had sliced them so thin, it only took a few minutes until he picked up the pan and tonged the zucchini onto a large serving platter.

"There," he said angrily and lifted the lid off another pan he'd been poaching salmon in. Using a thin spatula, he delicately transfered the three pieces he'd cooked onto the bed of veggie-noodles. The remainder of the sauce he carefully spooned on top of the already amazing fish. The minute he set the pan down, Professor Verminmeister walked around us and stepped in front of our station.

"That smells delicious, Mr. Nishimura."

"*Arigato*."

"May I?"

Roki pulled a clean fork out of our drawer and handed it to the professor. She pried a flake of fish off the corner, scooped a little of the zucchini, and popped it all into her cavernous mouth. Her eyes widened, and she beamed at Roki.

"Amazing. That might be the best salmon I've ever had. Should you ever find yourself without," she paused to cast me a disdainful look, "a need to look after those who cannot take care of themselves, you would have a brilliant future as a chef."

"Thank you, Professor." Roki gave her a little bow.

I bent below the counter and made gagging noises. "Sorry. hairball," I said as I sat up.

The disdainful look she flashed me earlier was nothing compared to the seething disgust and snide smile she held for a few moments and then walked away.

"Bitch."

"What was that, Miss Tanaka?"

"I said my butt had a twitch."

"That's strange. I didn't see you thinking." She cackled and walked away. Good thing, too. I was drunk enough to start some shit.

"Are you hungry?" Roki asked, sympathetically.

I looked down at the plate of food, ignored the whining from my tummy and flicked him off. "No. You don't get to be pissed, treat me like an asshole, even if I do deserve it, and then be nice. Fuck this place. I'm outta here."

Standing, Roki backed away from me and knocked over whatever bottle of booze he'd used in the sauce for the salmon. It splashed all over him and quickly spread to the

148

lit burner. Time slowed as I watched the flames lick the liquid and blue flames spread over the counter. Flashfire leapt from there to Roki's pants, igniting them instantly.

I screeched and without thinking, leapt at him, knocking him to the ground and smothering the flames with the only thing I had. Me. It burned and was stubborn, but I held onto his legs and smeared myself over him like a cheap whore.

I had just extinguished the last of them when Professor Velheim sprayed the two of us with a fire extinguisher. *Then* she turned it on the flames burning off on the counter.

"Miss Tanaka?"

"Yes, Professor?"

"Get out of my class."

"Yes, Professor." Covered in scorch marks, soot, and white powder, I stood and stared down at my ruined uniform. It vaguely reminded me of one night of clubbing in LA that I had *almost* forgotten. I smiled, twirled, and headed for the door.

"Professor, it was me who knocked over the bottle," Roki said in my defense.

"Roki, that girl is a hot mess and a danger to everybody around her. You included."

Tears streamed down my face. She wasn't wrong. Kicking open the door, I pulled off my jacket and left the class. The feeling of being watched made me pause and turn. I caught the worried looks of Fress and Kottr just as the door slammed shut.

∞ ∞ ∞

There was something therapeutic about taking a shower when I should have been in gym class. Pulling my bottle of mead out of the shampoo holder, I took a swig and put my head back under the water, letting it wash away the miasma of shitty day that was clinging to me like cheap perfume.

Reaching over blindly, I turned the water temperature even hotter, reached up and adjusted the head, turned around and slid down the wall until I was sitting on the wet tile. The stream was perfect, dumping abundant amounts of water on me while I sat on the floor and drank. I didn't even have to lean that far over to avoid getting my mead watered down. I smiled to myself as the shower washed away the tears that were steadily falling down my face.

You need to stop drinking.

Fenrir! What's up, buddy?

There was a moment of silence while he pondered on how to respond to my unusual outburst.

You go back to sleep?

I am always asleep. It is the outermost spheres of my dreams that brush your mind.

You gots some purdy fucked up dreams.

As do you. The one you had last night with your protector and the bucket of chicken was quite disturbing.

To you. I got off on that shit. Woke up sweating and shaking.

I know. Do you not think you have wallowed in self-pity long enough? You are going to lose consciousness.

Great thing about this school? Endless fucking hot water. At least I won't freeze my ass off. I took another drink and then ended up shaking the bottle when the last splash hit my tongue. "Fuck. Outta booze."

That is probably a good thing.

Good thing I knows peoples. I chuckled and held the bottle under the shower, letting it fill and then whispering a little prayer that it wouldn't be H2O with my next sip.

Fenrir didn't disappoint. Apparently, he wasn't awake enough to cut me off. I raised the bottle up in a silent toast. Or so I thought. The bottle flew from my hand, banged open the stall door, and bounced against the wall across the bathroom. Most of the mead splashed out upon impact, and the rest gurgled out of the bottle as it rolled over the floor toward the drain.

"Nooooo! That's alcohol abuse."

You cannot find me if you are dead.

Yeah, well you can bite me. That was the only *damn thing stopping my heart and head from hurting.* I leaned over and lay on my side, staring at the empty bottle as it finally settled.

You need to get up, my herald.

Don't wanna. I'm comfy and nobody wants me, anyway. Even Roki would be better without me.

Perhaps. But you can do nothing about changing lying on the floor of a water closet.

Water closet?

I felt him rummage around my head for the right word. *Shower.*

Fine. If you won't shut up, I might as well get dressed and go get drunker somewhere else. I rolled onto my stomach and got up on my knees, hanging onto the wall as I stood up slowly. Turning off the water, I pressed my forehead against the cold tile on the wall and stared down at my feet. "Don't fail me now," I whispered and shuffled around. Reaching for my towel, I stretched a bit too far and my foot slipped out from beneath me. My head struck the wall, and I watched in horrid fascination as the floor flew up to my face.

Muffled voices above me woke me up, and my head was propped against something soft instead of cold, hard tile.

"Owww," I groaned in agony. My head felt like a split melon, and my back and shoulder weren't much better.

"Are you okay? I feared the worst." Hiroki's voice caught, and I could feel the anguish in his words.

"Been better, been worse. Anybody got an aspirin?" Without opening my eyes, I started to sit up, but Roki's hand on my shoulder stopped me.

"Be still. The nurse is coming."

"She's gonna get sick of seeing me."

"We're going to swat you for running off alone. Again. Please stop doing that."

I cracked an eye and looked up at the other speaker. Flicking Rome off, I closed the eye letting way too much light into my head. "You don't get to tell me what to do anymore. You lost that right."

"Silence, Kaede-*sama*. He is the one who found you and called the rest of us."

Opening my eye, I squinted at the other two standing on the other side of the shower entrance. "Hey, guys." The pain slowed my thoughts a little, and what Roki said finally sank in. I narrowed my eyes at Rome. "How did you find me, passed out on the floor of the women's restroom? Hang out in here often?"

He sighed, shook his head, and left.

"No. Another student saw you on the floor, naked and bleeding, and screamed. Rome-*sama* was in the hallway."

"Oh. That makes sense."

I snuggled against Roki's leg and ignored everything around me, except for the warmth of the bathrobe someone had draped over me. Drifting in and out of slumber, I tried valiantly to ignore Roki's pleas for me to stay awake. When I finally opened my eyes again, I was lying in the infirmary bed. At the rate I was going, I probably should just have my belongings moved to the infirmary.

"Hello?"

It took a moment for Lornca to peek her head through the curtain. "How are you feeling?"

"Stellar. Got anything to drink?"

"Water?"

"Mead?"

"Water?"

"Water. Please." I groaned and put my arm over my eyes, blocking the overhead lights from melting my brain.

She returned with a plastic cup filled with clear liquid. I gave a silent prayer to Fenrir for a little transubstantiation magic, but he ignored me. For once. I should have been grateful, but it just pissed me off.

Hmmph.

He was definitely ignoring me.

"What happened?"

"Everybody hates me. Got drunk and fell down."

She reached for my forehead and just before her palm connected with my skin, it started glowing green and felt warm to the touch. She sat silently for a moment and then nodded, pulling her hand away. "The swelling is down, and your wound is healed."

"Put your hand back? That felt good."

She sighed, pulled the chair over to the bed, and sat down next to me. "I hate to break I to you, but your headache isn't from your injury. It's from your damn drinking. I'm cautioning you to stop."

Ignoring her, I closed my eyes and pretended to dose off. If I had a dollar for every time someone had urged me to quit drinking, I'd be richer than my parents.

"I'm not telling you to do this for you. I'm begging you to do it for those around you."

"Afraid I'll get tanked and run off to find Fenrir?"

"Not in the slightest. After spending some time with you and getting to know you, I don't think you could find him if you wanted to. I'm seriously surprised you can find your way back to your room each night." She stood up and headed for the curtain.

"Ouch." I opened my eyes and stared at her in shock. "Thought people in the medical industry were supposed to be all kind and helpful."

"Not when their patience with patients is at an all-time low. You have nobody to blame but yourself for this one, and the only person you truly hurt was your friends. Especially Hiroki."

"Hiroki? He's used to my shenanigans."

She spun and gave me a look of utter hatred. Stepping toward me, I held up my hands thinking I was going to have to fend off an attack, but she just lowered her face closer to mine and whispered in my ear, "But he's not used to you forgetting his birthday." She straightened and let her words sink in.

My already broken heart just shattered. There wasn't a piece big enough left to fit in a thimble. I'd completely done it and gotten so self-absorbed that I decimated the one person who'd always been there for me and *never*, not once, let me down. I was a shit, scum, and didn't deserve to be on the same continent as him. No wonder he'd been so passive aggressively pissed at me all morning. I couldn't blame him, either. If he had *ever* forgotten about *my* birthday…

"He thinks it's his fault you slipped in the shower, you know. You should have seen him when I got there, pacing the floor, crying out in terror. He even threw up. He thought because he was angry with you, you stormed off and drank yourself stupid."

"That would be Hiroki." I choked back a sob.

"Don't worry. I calmly explained to him that you were stupid before you started drinking."

"Thank you." I actually meant it. Maybe Roki would listen to the school nurse and actually realize I wasn't worth a shit.

Rolling over, I pulled the blanket over my head and let the tears start falling. I was almost a little shocked that I even had any left.

"You going to wallow in self-misery? Or are you going to go show him how much he means to you and grow up, Kaede?"

I stuck my arm out from under the covers and waved it in the air. "The self-misery part," I mumbled from under the covers.

"I figured," she answered with a sigh, pulling open my curtain and leaving me there alone, like I wanted.

As soon as I heard the curtain close, I got up and opened the window by my bed as quietly as possible. The ancient wood frame didn't make it easy to be silent, but I managed. As soon as it was open, I shifted, letting the fox loose and leaping through the opening.

Before my paws touched the ground, I popped to the closest building and skirted the edge by the shrubbery, my mostly white fur blending in perfectly with the snow. It took me nearly fifteen minutes to finally reach the boundaries of the academy property and slip into the forest beyond.

I was finished as a student, a friend, and a lover. All of them would be better off without me. I'd live as a fox in the wild for a few weeks, until they stopped searching for me, and their memories of me started to fade. Maybe they'd even be relieved I was gone. One thing was for certain, I needed to find a way across the ocean. The odds of me waking Fenrir in Iceland were slim to none. The odds of me doing it from California were nil.

Chapter 14

Just because I had caught the mouse, and killed the mouse, didn't mean I wanted to eat the mouse. But after two days without food and only snow to keep me hydrated, I had little choice. Lowering my face to its tiny broken body, I gingerly picked it up between my teeth and flipped it into the air, catching it and swallowing it whole.

I'm sure if I could have seen myself, my fur would have been green with disgust. A shiver ran down my spine as the mouse slithered down my gullet. "That's fucking disgusting."

Oh. And I was talking to myself. Two days was forty-seven hours longer than I'd ever gone without talking to somebody or without supervision. I was going a little batty, and I'm sure if somebody had come across a fox talking to themselves in the middle of the forest, they would have shot first and asked questions with a Ouija board later.

I was still hungry. But not for more Lil Mickeys. I needed cheekin. Or a burger. Or an all you can eat buffet. Turning my head, I stared longingly toward the school and then toward the village of Oddi. Either would have been preferable to vermin al fresco.

Running away wasn't the smartest thing I had ever done and that was saying a *lot*.

It was the weekend. The guys were most likely in the village either looking for me or drinking away their memories of the stupid little white-headed fox that made their lives miserable. *Maybe, I can sneak back into the school and filch a quick meal...*

Maybe you should just go back.

Oh! Look who's back. Not a peep out of you for almost three days.

You were not in the mood for interaction.

Still not.

You are starving and a blizzard is approaching. You will not survive the night.

Fear crept up my spine and dissipated almost immediately. *I can live with that.*

No. You cannot. I have shielded you from the others to give you some time to appreciate them a little more and to calm your nerves. It is time to go back to your school, Little Fox.

Not so foxy anymore, thanks to you. I look like a fucking husky.

My power is seeping into you. It cannot be helped. Soon you will be my little wolf.

But I like being a fox!

You will appreciate the power.

Nope. Not a fan. It goes to your head.

You do not have a choice.

Oh, Fenrir. You silly little thing, you. Yes, I do.

Hmmmph. So, you say. Your Geri is leading your men to you. Stay put, it will make it easier to find you.

Not if I run.

I leapt from where I sat, landing a few feet away and pumping my legs as fast as they could carry me across the snow-covered slopes. Unfortunately, I was running uphill, but if they were going to chase me, so would they.

I command you to stop!

I command you to suck my butt.

Pain exploded in my vision as invisible jaws clamped down on my neck, forcing my head to plow into the snow.

158

The pain came from the tattoos on my face flaring into life once again, illuminating the snow around me in an eerie blue light. Even under my dense fur, they still glowed brightly.

I said stop.

I said suck my butt.

The invisible jaws around my neck tightened, making breathing damn near impossible. If I kept insulting him, I'd either end the day asphyxiated or frozen. A win either way.

You would rather die than admit to those you love you were behaving badly? You are insane.

Did you just meet me? I'm not doing it to punish them...I'm doing it to punish me. I suck. I blow. I'm no good at the relationship thing. I piss everybody off, make them miserable, and can't seem to focus on anything but me! I've been like this my whole fucking life, and I'm sick of it.

So, change.

I can't! Don't you think I've fucking tried? It wasn't until that moment that I learned foxes could cry. Not just tears dripping down our fur covered cheeks, like full on little yippy sobs, whining ugly cries.

Little Fox, you can do anything *you set your mind to. Except escape me. Do not try. I won't punish you. I will kill the ones you love. Keep that in mind.*

There was a bit of a crunch and a spurt of blood from my neck as his spectral teeth pierced my flesh. It wasn't enough to do any serious damage, just enough to remind me that his little fox was his little bitch.

Shall I demonstrate on your Geri? Or, perhaps, on one of your lovers. The fox?

No! Don't you fucking dare. I won't kill myself, but if you ever *hurt any of them, I will lemur myself off the first fucking cliff I can find. Deal?*

There was a crack of thunder and he said, *Deal.*

Two werewolves, two hellhounds, and a brown fox broke through the trees into the clearing where I'd been making my getaway. Fenrir didn't let go of me until I was surrounded.

Roki was the first to shift, staring at me with anguish in his eyes and a trembling lip, almost afraid to close the distance between us. Maybe he could still feel Fenrir's spirt atop me. Finally, worry outweighed caution, and he walked forward, dropping to the ground beside me. As soon as his knees crunched the snow, the grip on my neck was gone.

Shifting, I lay there in the snow, wearing nothing but the hospital gown and staring up at my Roki with sadness and sorrow threatening to finish off my already shattered heart. All I could do was nod at him. I didn't even move when he scooped me out of the snow and held me to his chest, hot tears dripping on my cheeks.

"You damn fool."

"Roki?"

"What?"

"Help me."

He gulped and held me tighter, answering me with long slow nods. Finally giving a soft chuckle and pressing his lips to my ear. "That was not so hard, was it?"

∞ ∞ ∞

I'd refused to let them take me to the infirmary, opting for a hot shower and to be tucked into bed by three of them. Rome had excused himself to let Uncle Tatsuo know that I had been found. Geri gave me one last relieved look and then a sneer of disgust before heading back to her room. I'd forgotten that if I died, she died. I might have been thinking about killing myself there for a minute, but I wasn't a murderer. Even if she was a bitch ninety-nine-point-nine percent of the time.

160

"Why?" Remy's question caught me off guard.

I blinked at him a few times and finally gave up trying to think of a reason and shrugged my shoulders.

His face contorted in anger, and he strode to the bed, putting his faces inches from mine and snarling almost incomprehensibly. "No! You don't get to shrug this off, Kaede! You almost died. We have been sick with worry for the past two days. Why? Because Rome was trying to comfort you by pretending to be me? Because you forgot it was your lover's birthday? Why? We deserve an answer!" He slammed his open hand down on the bed next to me. Roki took a step closer, but didn't interfere. David even nodded and moved closer.

"Because."

"Use your words, Kaede," Remy said, a little calmer.

"Everything. I was so angry at Rome, Roki was pissed at me, and then Lornca went ham on my ass, and something broke inside me. I was tired of hurting and hurting everybody else because I suck at living."

Remy sighed and sat down on the bed next to me, leaning back against the bed and offering me his chest to lean against. As soon as I rolled onto his arm, he wrapped it around my shoulder and kissed the top of my head. "You don't suck at anything," he paused and let out a little bark of laughter. "Except what you're supposed to suck at." He gave me a wink and squeezed me a little tighter.

"I do. If you look up the definition of self-centered brat in the dictionary, there's a police sketch of me next to it."

"Only because you've been spoiled until this moment." He shot Roki a nasty glare, and my best friend in the world actually nodded in agreement.

"I am to blame, without a doubt."

"Shut yer trap, Roki. No, you're not. I am. Totally."

He shrugged, and I let it go, an argument for another day.

"Well, I am sure the two of you have much to discuss. Thank you, Kaede."

"For what?"

"Not dying. I don't think I could have handled that," Remy answered, uncharacteristically tender. He kissed the top of my head again and then lowered his head a little more and gently caressed my lips with his. He flashed me one more warm smile and frowned at me again. "I mean it. If you're having problems, talk to us. No more running away." He bonked my head playfully and stood. "David?"

He nodded and crept over to the bed and bent over, pulling me into his arms and sighing in relief. "I'll see you tomorrow. Get some rest, and spend some time with Hiroki."

"I will." I hugged him back and kissed him.

The two of them left, and it was just Roki and I. The silence was awkward, and he was shuffling around the room, picking up this and straightening that. I even waited patiently while he organized his sock drawer, watching him the whole time.

Finally, with nothing else to clean or organize, he sat down on his bed, facing me. "Kaede-*sama*…"

I held out my arms to him, and he stood, practically running into them and lying on top of me, face pressed into my neck as sobs wracked his body. Stroking his hair, I whispered, "Shhhh. It's okay," over and over until the sobbing stopped.

He wasn't asleep, but he refused to move until the weight of him became a little too much to bear, and I wiggled under him. "Do you need me to move?" I could barely hear him, he whispered so softly.

"I can't feel my toes." I giggled to let him know I was teasing, but he rolled us onto our sides and hugged me tightly against him. "This would be a lot more fun if we were nekkid."

"You are in no condition to–"

It was amazing how quickly he shut up with a mouthful of my tongue. We kissed for a few moments before I reached down between us and started lifting his shirt up over his chiseled stomach, dragging my fingertips over his muscles as I did. I pulled away from that kiss and motioned for him to get it the rest of the way off.

"Are you sure?"

"What? We're not going to do anything. Naked therapeutic cuddles are an actual thing. I'm still a little cold, so I'm going to steal some of your body heat." It sounded perfectly plausible to me.

"Uh huh." He chuckled and pulled the shirt over his head. I seized the opportunity to take my thin T-shirt and boxers off. He paused to admire my body from toes to nose and let *his* fingers trail over my stomach. "Beautiful."

I blushed and muttered, "And you're still overdressed. Get those pants off so we can get under the covers."

"*Hai, Ojo-sama.*"

"You're gonna spoil me if you keep calling me Princess."

"*Hai.* I shall continue to spoil you and treat you like a queen. Because you are to me."

I opened my mouth to protest, but he silenced me with a finger over my lips. "But, I do promise to let you know when you are being an ass. And if you continue to not listen to my sage advice, I shall bind you and stuff you in a closet. Deal?"

I grinned and nodded. Now I would just have to fight the urge to misbehave to get him to tie me up. The thought of that sent tingles in places that liked that thought even more than I did. "Please?"

He chuckled and unbuttoned his pants, bending at his waist to get them over his ass and down his legs. The angle put his lips perilously close to my nipples and he kissed

163

each one of them gently. They sprang to life, as did Little Roki…

"You better not be getting too hard. We're just snuggling," I reminded him with a wink.

"If that is your wish."

"For now. I want to feel you."

He slipped his arm under me and rolled me over on top of him, somehow also pulling the cover over us and turning off the light. The moon was filtering into our room, illuminating us in silver blue light. "Like this?"

"Perfect," I whispered happily and pressed my face against his chest as he lazily let the tips of his fingers slide up and down my back, stopping just short of touching my butt. "Yes, you are." I nodded for emphasis.

His fingers stopped moving, and a subtle sigh escaped his chest. "No. If I were perfect, I would have seen how you were struggling and not let my frustration affect my behavior."

"Roki?"

"Yes, Kaede-*sama?*"

"I don't know if you know this, but I'm not the brightest twinkle in the sky. I'm so sorry I forgot it was your birthday." I sniffed, fighting back the tears that were threatening to leak out all over him.

"It is not important. I was being dense myself. And you are correct, you are not a twinkle in the night sky, you are the moon. You are everything to me and always have been. Again, I apologize."

I shut him up with another kiss. It bothered me when Roki apologized because he *never* did anything wrong. I meant it when I told him he was perfect. When I pulled away, I smiled at him. "I've forgotten your birthday before, you were always amused by it and tortured me for weeks for forgetting. Is it because we are lovers that it bothered you this time?"

164

Even in the moonlight, I could see his cheeks redden in embarrassment. I'd hit the nail on the head. "*Hai*," he answered meekly.

"Well, since we are lovers…I should give you an *extra* special birthday present, shouldn't I?"

"You do not have to, *Ojo-sama.*"

"Princesses don't suck the cocks of their most bestest friends." I grinned and pushed the covers off.

"Kaede…"

"Roki…," I mimicked and got up on my knees and carefully maneuvered myself until I was facing the opposite direction and kneeling over his stomach. He was already proud and hard when I lowered myself onto his rippling muscles and took him into my hands. "You protested, but Little Roki seems so happy to see me."

"As am I," he said, his hands gently rubbing my hips.

"Oh, you want to see me? Is that what you're saying?" I giggled and looked over my shoulder at him, laughing harder at the smile on his face as he stared at my bare ass. "See something you like?"

He glanced up at me and wiggled his eyebrows before feasting his gaze back on my ass.

I leaned forward, exposing myself to him, and slid back closer to his face. His cock surged in excitement, and then I squealed when he grabbed my hips and pulled me *all* the way back. "Um. I'm supposed to be blowing you…"

"No reason for one of us to have all the fun." He blew a puff of breath across my already rapidly moistening lips and then kissed the covering over my clit, letting his tongue flicker out to push down my hood. I hissed in pleasure and kissed the tip of his cock. He kissed my lips and let his tongue slide between them, and just when he reached the top, he kept going.

As his tongue danced across the sensitive flesh between my openings, I pulled his tip into my mouth and swirled my tongue completely around his trapped head and then suckled it. He groaned and let his tongue venture farther north, tracing the outside of my forbidden zone.

Pulling him from my mouth, I looked back and moaned. "What are you doing?"

"Leaving nothing unexplored."

"But that's…"

"I know precisely what it is, Kaede-*sama*. There is no part of you I do not wish to lavish with kisses."

"Pretty sure that was your tongue."

"Would you prefer my lips?"

"No…"

One finger reached under me and slipped just inside my pussy, gathering some of my juices before he started making circles around my clit as his tongue danced across my other hole.

Breathing became very difficult, and I turned my head back around, determined to repay the pleasure. I reached forward and grabbed his thighs, lifting them off the bed and parting his legs. His cock throbbed in front of me, and I sucked him back into my mouth as I put my arms over his thighs and gripped his cock with one hand and his balls with the other.

We were locked in a classic sixty-nine position and in a desperate battle to make the other come first.

He took the lead when he plunged his other finger in my pussy for lubrication and then swirled it over my puckered butthole and then poked his tongue inside. I was forced to pull his cock from my mouth and hiss as pleasure like I had never experienced before caused every muscle below my waist to contract. "Fuuuck."

"You like?"

"Don't stop."

I tackled his cock again, forcing it to go deeper into my throat than I ever had before. We were in uncharted waters, and I gagged as I went a little too far. The reflex must have caused him pleasure, because his ass lifted slightly off the bed. I gripped his balls a little tighter and rolled them gently together. His hip thrusts came a little faster as he involuntarily tried to fuck my mouth. I grinned around him and *sucked*. Sucked like I was trying to drain every drop from him, which I was.

He again got the upper hand when he shoved two fingers in my pussy with the fingers that had been teasing my clit, scooped some more juices with his other, and then slipped it inside my anus. It was pleasurable beyond belief, but when his fingers touched each other with only the walls between them, I saw little floating stars as an orgasm ripped through me. My ass thrust backward, and his teeth grazed the flesh of my ass, biting down gently as he fingered both of my holes. I breathed through my nose, his cock still throbbing in my mouth when he started cumming. His hips bucked as I suckled every drop from him, not swallowing, but holding it between my ever-expanding cheeks.

When he was finished, he gently pulled his fingers from me, and I turned around, straddling his hips and leaning in for a kiss. When his lips parted, I shared his gift to me with him, and that kiss turned into the dirtiest, nastiest, best kiss in the history of kisses. We devoured each other for minutes until we both needed to breathe.

"Woah," I said happily, resting my head on his shoulder as I collapsed on top of him.

"That was… Yes. I liked that very much."

I bounced as Roki chuckled.

"Hey, Roki?"

"*Hai?*"

"In case I've never said it enough, I love you."

"As I love and adore you, Kaede-*sama*."

167

I smiled happily and wiggled against him, breathing in his spicy scent and feeling thoroughly loved. I truly was an idiot. It might take a few days, but I needed to apologize to everyone. Preferably in the same way. *Maybe a group apology would be better...*

I was mentally giggling when I felt Roki's cock nudge my entrance. Lifting my head, I gave him an incredulous look.

He shrugged. "Sorry."

"Don't be. I was just surprised. Happy birthday, Roki," I said, smiled, and pushed myself back against his very rigid cock. He slipped right inside me, and I breathed out in happiness as I fully enveloped him.

We didn't fuck. Not after that sixty-nine. That was our playful time. We made love slowly, grinding against each other and just letting the pleasure fill in what was missing like an ooey-gooey chocolate cake after a large meal. We had our dessert, and we came at the same time with me whispering his name repeatedly, and him filling my pussy with his hot cum. We didn't even clean up. We were happy and satiated.

"Love you," I repeated as I dozed off, smiling at the feeling of him still inside me.

"I love you more, Kaede-*sama.*"

Chapter 15

Tucking a strand of still damp hair behind my ear, I checked my uniform one last time while waiting for Roki to finish tying his last shoe. It was a monumental occasion; I was ready before him. Granted, he had woken up very happy with me on top of him, and I wasn't one to let such an advantage go... I may have worn him out a little and made us a little later than usual. Totally worth it though.

"Will you hurry up? I've been ready for *hours...*"

"It's your fault. You should not be so enticing when you first wake up. I could hardly say no." He gave me a warm smile over his shoulder that made me happy. And a bit squishy.

Fuck me, how can he be so sexy and not burst into flames? Maybe he has fire retardant underpants. I shifted and debated changing mine. At least I didn't have to worry about *them* catching on fire. Steaming me like a lobster, maybe. Spontaneously combusting, no.

He finished and stood up, motioning for me to head to class. If we didn't hurry, we were going to be late for Finance class, but our teacher was the coolest one we had. She'd let us off the hook. Especially if Roki batted his eyes at her.

Opening the door and bursting out into the hallway, I crashed into Fress' side and yelped. "Sorry!"

"Kaede?" Fress stared at me wide-eyed and turned, pressing his forehead against mine and turning his head to rub his cheek down mine.

"We had feared the worst, but finally felt you when you returned last night." Kottr's voice was deep, but I could still hear the elation in his voice. He moved forward and repeated Fress' face rubs. It was awkward, and I didn't know how I felt about two hot gay guys rubbing their faces against me, but I just chalked it up to them being feline in nature. The gesture did seem kind of catty. Not in the bitchy way, more like the Friskies way.

Roki put his arms around me from behind, somewhat shielding me from their affections. "We should get to class," he rumbled behind me.

"If I may? I need to speak with Kaede for a moment," Fress said, stepping back and giving us enough space to completely move into the hallway and shut our door.

Roki gave me a questioning glance, and I nodded almost imperceptibly. I could see his desire to do as I asked warring with the fear of leaving me alone. "Come, Kottr. Let us get to class and let the professor know they shall be late."

"Ja."

Roki was worried about me being alone with the kitties. I was more worried about Roki being alone with Kottr. The handsome, gray-haired youthful looking whatever he was seemed a little *too* happy to be alone with my boyfriend. I was waiting for him to grab onto Roki's arm and giggle as they walked. My worry didn't go unnoticed by Fress, either. He chuckled when I finally looked at him.

"Do not worry. He is faithful to me."

"But Roki is hot."

"So are you, and yet I trust myself to be alone with you."

170

"But you're gay."

He sighed and shook his head. "Even those that claim to be straight can be persuaded by what is inside a person."

"Well, then you're safe with me."

"Do not underestimate yourself, Kaede. You are as beautiful inside as you are out, you are just young. Great beauty comes with age."

"Is that why there is such a huge difference between my mother and me?"

"Most likely. I cannot see her holding a candle to your looks, though."

"Are you into red-heads?" I chuckled. "S'watcha wanna talk to me about?"

"Just a word of caution. When you have the gift of Seidr…you must chose your words very carefully."

"Uhhh…the whosamawatcher Freya gave me?"

"Ja."

"You know what it is?"

He laughed. "You do not?"

"Um… No?"

"Seidr. Fate magic. You could have hurt your boyfriend pretty badly in class the other day. Luckily the professor sprayed you with that powder."

"Wait, what?"

"When your lover caught on fire?"

"You're saying that really *was* my fault?"

"I believe your words were, 'Liar, liar, pants on fire?'"

I could almost hear the *wah, wah, waah* of a trombone in the distance. "Holy fuckballs. I could have killed him." I stared incredulously at Fress. "Next time, lead with that? Why am I just finding out about it now?"

"We assumed our goddess informed you of its power."

"No. She didn't. But in her defense, I was being pretty annoying. Dying takes a lot out of a girl." I held up my hand and stared at him in shock.

"What is it?"

"Remind me never to use the phrase, 'Fuck me,' ever again."

He rolled his eyes and shook his head. "I do not think it works like that. You have the power to affect the fates of those around you, not get laid."

"Whew. Cuz if I'm being honest, I'm a little sore right now."

"I believe this is the part where I say, 'Too much information.'"

"Shush. You know you were totally interested."

"Perhaps."

"Fress?"

"Yes?"

"Why the fuck would she give this power to me? Doesn't she realize how hopelessly irresponsible I am?"

"More than likely. But she also probably gave it to you because you will have great need of it in the coming times."

"Ragnarok?"

"Not if we can help it."

"Come on. Let's get to class. I don't want Roki to worry about you and me."

"You're just tired of worrying about him and Kottr."

"Maybe."

∞ ∞ ∞

I resisted the urge to smack my face down on the desk and start snoring loudly. There were few things as boring as Human Government, the class however, was a thousand times worse. Ten minutes in, I started dozing off. Twenty, I felt myself slipping into a coma. Forty minutes in, and my cells starting to lose their cohesive bonding, and I felt myself becoming one with the universe. Ten minutes left, and I regretted ever being born.

It took thirty-seven years for the last ten minutes of class to finally pass. Why they subjected us to Human Government was beyond me. I didn't see any of us going into politics after graduation. The humans were lucky we obeyed their laws at all. Most of the time. And when we did, it was to avoid getting outed as something *other* than human. It was a delicate balance, but it had worked for almost five-hundred years. The last witch hunt was when we gave up trying to stand out and "blend in" became our motto.

I heard there was a town somewhere in Virginia where supernatural creatures lived out in the open among humans…but it sounded like a big pile of steamy bullshit to me. Roki wanted to look for the place one day, but it seemed a little too much like work to me.

The bell jolted me awake, and I smiled at everyone around me, ignoring the disgruntled look of the teacher, Professor James. Luckily, I understood the ins and outs of human government. One of the added perks of your parents owning a whole town. They kept it as normal as possible, and it was one of the few things that I had picked up tagging along with them as a small child. When Roki and I weren't setting things on fire. Me mostly, but he was guilty by association. I was passing Human Government with flying colors. I think it was the reason the teacher hated me. One of them.

"Lunch!" I grinned at Hiroki. "That's my favorite class."

"And you are acing it, Kaede-*sama.*"

"Come on. It's Salisbury Steak Day!"

"She seems in a better mood," one of the other students mumbled under their breath to another student. I had no idea of either of their names. Making an effort to fit in a little better might be a good idea. We still had two-and-a-half years left of school, and people got pissed off when you referred to them as "Other student."

I did it anyway. "Yes, I am, Other Student." I even nodded.

"Somebody got laid," another other student muttered.

"Yes, I–" Roki's hand covered my mouth from behind.

"Forgive her. It's time for her medication."

There were chuckles all around as he practically dragged me from class by my tiny little head. When we were through the door, I finally tapped out, slapping his arm repeatedly until he gave me the opportunity to breath.

"We need a safe word."

"You couldn't speak anyway."

"Hand signal then. Don't know if you know this about me, but I kinda need oxygen."

"You seemed to be doing fine last night..." He grinned, totally proud of himself.

"Yeah, your cock isn't that restricting."

"Ouch." He gave me a little pout.

"Hey. Your hand is huge. It's called fisting for a reason." I slapped his arm and giggled. "So, hand signal. I hold up four fingers, and you let go."

"No. Four is strike low and take the head. You always forget that one."

"Five?"

"This person attacked me in a sexual nature. Make him a eunuch."

"Three?"

"That is to call me."

"Two?"

"I need a fire extinguisher and a twinkie. We haven't used that one in over a year. Rewrite?"

"Rewrite. Now it's let me breathe."

"*Hai.*"

174

"Now I want a twinkie."

"You will have to settle for cheesecake."

"Cheesecake is never settling. It's an upgrade. Grand prize. The end all, be all of existence."

"I do not care for it."

We stopped walking, only partway to the Dining Hall. "Roki… I don't think we can be lovers anymore."

"Maybe it was your cheesecake I did not like. I shall try the school's."

"Wait! You mean to tell me the cheesecake I made for you in seventh grade is the only one you have ever tried?"

He blushed, nodded, and started walking again. I rushed to catch up and grabbed his arm.

"Seriously?"

"Kaede-*sama*, I do not know how to tell you this…"

"It was that gross?"

"I do not think because it has the word cheese in the name, you are allowed to substitute whatever kind you could find."

"That was imported Parmigiano Reggiano."

"That was disgusting."

"But you ate the whole thing!"

"Of course. You made it for me."

A lump formed in my throat that I was having trouble swallowing. I coughed and stumbled a little, overwhelmed by his sweetness. "Well, next birthday, I'm going to make you another cheesecake, the right way."

"Muenster?"

"I'm thinking Colby-Jack. It has a nice mellow finish and goes good with Chili."

He chuckled and patted my arm. "I look forward to it."

"I just hope all this gods and Ragnarok bullshit will be over with by then."

"Let us focus on keeping your sleeping god slumbering away peacefully."

"He will wake whether it is by my hand or not. He shall rise before the end of winter and unleash his vengeance. It is up to us to slay the beast."

"Kaede?"

We had stopped walking, and there wasn't a sound around us. I'd been staring down the corridor when the words slipped from my lips like prophetic honey. "Lyrics to an old song," I lied and plastered a smile on my face.

He nodded slowly, giving me the benefit of the doubt. I just forced myself to breathe and started heading for the Dining Hall again. Nothing a little Salisbury Steak couldn't fix. Maybe a small drink…

"Are you all right?"

"Honky dory, peachy keen. Why? Don't I look all right?"

"Just a strange…vibe? As you would say."

"Nope. Just hungry. Nerd some ferd."

"You're always hungry and need some food."

"Your Ermagerdian is horrible. I could barely understand your accent."

He rolled his eyes and pulled the door open. "Lerdies ferst."

I grinned and squealed. "Erky derky, Hirerki." I booped his nose and practically ran into the cafeteria, snagging a couple of trays and handing one to Roki.

"How would you say cheesecake in Ermagerdian?"

"Cherzkerk."

"I am sorry I asked." He motioned me to the buffet with a nod and look.

In an effort to turn over a new leaf, I took a small side salad. No reason the leaf couldn't be romaine. "I'm eating a salad. Ain'tcha proud?"

"Positively ecstatic," he answered drolly, almost worriedly.

We filled our plates, and by plates, I meant one for Hiroki and two for me. He took a selection of grilled chicken and veggies, with just a small bowl of rice. I opted for taters, gravy, and four beef patties smothered in more gravy. Whatever scientist that developed the food pyramid should have his medical license stripped for not giving gravy its own category.

Heading for the beverages, Roki set his tray on the counter and grabbed two glasses. "Tea?"

"Coke."

He raised his eyebrow.

"Don't judge me. Blood sugar is low, and I need to counteract the benefits of the salad."

"Baby steps."

"Yep."

"Get us a table?"

"Kay."

I spotted David and the twins already seated and stuffing their faces. David raised his arm, and I gulped, plastering another smile on my face and heading for them. "Hey, beautiful."

"Handsome. Handsome, too. Dickface."

Remy frowned, but quickly changed it to a smile of greeting. Rome just grunted and continued eating, not even looking up from his plate.

In two-point-three seconds, I'd completely killed the mood at the table. *Slick, Kaede.*

I set my tray down and walked around the table until I was standing next to Rome. "Look, I suck at apologies, but that was really rude. I'm sorry."

He nodded and finally looked up at me. "It's okay."

"No, it's not. In fact, I've been a complete shit lately, and I'm trying not to be. So, if I ever do anything like that again, please yell at me or something so I know I'm being an asshole."

177

"Can I draw a dick on your forehead in Sharpie?"

"Sure."

He smiled and nodded, returning to his food. "Thank you," He mumbled in return. I turned to find Remy and David staring at me like I had a tail growing out of my forehead.

"What?"

"Who are you and what did you do with the real Kaede?" Remy actually slid his chair back a little in mock fear.

"Har har."

Hiroki showed up with our drinks and sat, shaking his head at the quivering mound of protein and carbs that wasn't going to eat itself. I walked around Rome and ran my fingers over David's shoulders as I passed.

"Joking aside, are you feeling okay?"

"Yes," I answered and sat. Picking up my fork, I cut a forkful of ground steak, smashed it into the taters, dipped it in gravy, and shoved it into my mouth. "I forgot corn!"

Remy laughed. "Sit. I'll get you some."

He got up and left before I could stop him. I mentally kicked myself. I wanted everybody to stop waiting on me all the time. Maybe we needed to have a town meeting to discuss my end of year resolutions.

"Kaede…"

"David?"

He paused a moment to gather his thoughts. "You uh…don't need to change. We liked you just the way you were."

"But that Kaede was a pain in the ass cheeks."

"But we adored her," Roki added.

Even Rome nodded.

"I'm trying to be a better person, and you guys don't want me to?"

Remy set a bowl of buttered corn in front of me. "No."

"Huh?" I looked up at him in shock. He went back to his seat and looked at the other three, who nodded at him silently.

They had some sort of ESP thing going on. "We had a talk…" Remy picked up his tea and took a sip, staring at me over the rim, letting his eyes meet mine.

The fork fell out of my hand. "You guys are breaking up with me?" I could barely breathe. Until I swallowed the mouthful of mashed potatoes I'd mumbled around. Then it came in ragged gasps.

"No!" The three of them I was actually dating shouted in unison.

Rome just finished his mouthful of food and stood up. "I should be going." He grabbed his tray and started walking toward the bussing station. The other three stared at me expectantly.

Sighing, I stopped him by calling his name. "Stay. Please?"

He dumped his tray in the container before sitting back down by his brother. He still refused to look up at me.

"Thank you."

His only response was a slight nod.

I looked around the table. "So, color me confused… I thought all of you were sick of me."

They shook their heads. "Why the hell would you think that?" Remy had become their impromptu spokesperson.

"Well, Roki was pissed off at me, I was fighting with Rome. I don't know. It was just too much, too fast. I got overwhelmed and freaked." I poked at my food with my fork. Not wanting to go on with any more reasoning for my psychotic break.

"Well, I can't speak for all of us," he paused and gave his brother a wry smile, "but I love you."

"I love you too, Kaede," David grinned and stroked my cheek.

"I have not tired of you at all. When you forgot my birthday, I was a little put off, but you know I can't stay mad at you, Kaede-*sama*."

I sniffled and forked a tiny bit of food into my mouth. When I looked up from my plate, Rome was actually staring at me. "What?"

"Do you want to know how I feel about you?"

"I can guess."

"You'd probably be wrong."

"I'll be happy if you don't hate me."

He let out a small huff of laughter. "No, Little Fox. I don't hate you. You're frustrating, vulgar, sometimes a nuisance. You constantly needle those around you, sometimes I question your sanity, sometimes I question mine."

"Gee, don't hold back. Tell me how you *really* feel."

"There isn't a damn thing about you that I would change, either. You're perfect the way you are. You're you."

The fork kind of fell out of my hand, and I jumped when it hit the side of the plate.

"You smell funny." Don't judge me, it was all I could come up with. "And you're a grump. And I don't like it when you lie."

He nodded.

"You really hurt me by pretending to be what you weren't."

"And you hurt me every time you thought I was my brother and kissed me."

"You liked it."

"Yeah. Just a little."

"I did have fun that night... Well, up until you got busted and all hell broke loose."

"I did, too. Wanna try it again?"

"Absolutely not. But I'd love to go out with Remy. Be a shame if his evil twin stood in for him." I gave him a wink.

He smirked and nodded. "I'll see if I can find some chloroform or something."

"Have him pick me up for dinner. It's Monday, so we should probably have dinner here. Remy and me, I meant."

"Of course."

The rest of the table watched our exchange with amused glances between Rome and me. Like they were watching a ping pong match.

The smile drained from my face. There was a peculiar feeling raising the hair on the back of my neck. The four of them stood and reached out, screams forming on their lips as everything around me slowed. The feeling intensified and pain seared my cheeks as my tattoos flared to life. Dodging to the right I ended up in Roki's arms just as the heavy axe smashed the chair I'd been sitting in. A frustrated scream tore from Sabine's little pocket dimension as she started to pull the axe back through.

Four hands erupted from around the tear in space, seizing Sabine and dragging her out kicking and screaming. It took a moment for Fress and Kottr to register to my senses. With a *pop*, the rift closed and the three of them stood there, Sabine panting heavily from swinging the hefty weapon and from thrashing against her captors.

"Fuck you! Let me go!"

"Sabine!" Rome roared and stood, walking around the table and ripping the axe from her grip.

I just stood there in shock as she looked at her brother with utter disgust and betrayal.

"Remy, go get the headmaster."

"I'd be delighted to," he said and took off running.

Finally, Sabine tore her gaze from her brother and snarled at me. All the pain and anguish she had ever caused me came crashing back, and I narrowed my eyes at her, stood, and punched her in the face as hard as I could.

I was about to go for seconds when Roki wrapped his arms around me from behind and whispered calmingly in my ear. "She is not worth it and can't harm you again."

Kottr and Fress nodded in agreement.

Sabine spit blood on the floor at my feet and looked up slowly, seeming happy. A little too happy. "Checkmate," she said with a giggle.

There was a ripping sound as another rift opened up behind me. The *swish* of a blade cutting through the air ended abruptly as it struck something solid. Sabine's face went from elated to horrified, and I spun just in time to see David, arms outstretched to protect me, fall to his knees. A wet gurgling sound bubbled from his front as the axe and arms disappeared into the rift.

David had jumped in front of me, shielding me with his own body just as Sabine's accomplice struck.

"David?" His name quivered off my lips.

He didn't answer, just fell face forward to the floor, knocking my chair on its side as he collapsed.

Sabine and I both screamed and watched in horror as blood began to pool around him. I dropped to the ground beside him, my heart in my throat.

"He's okay," I said, gripping his shoulder and rolling him over.

A vision of the first time he introduced himself to me flashed through my memory. His smile. His kindness, the sun shining on his brown hair. Flash forwarding to the time in the common room we had been naughty. Every moment of every time we spent alone. The first time we made love. Everything started crashing through my mind as his face came into view. I sobbed at his smile. It didn't go with his lifeless eyes as they stared up at the ceiling.

"David?" He didn't respond, just continued to stare up above me, the color draining from his face. "David. David. David!" I slapped his cheek. This was no time to be playing around. He was okay. He had to be. "David, stop fucking around!" I screamed, a wordless hollow echo from my heart.

Nobody moved around me. Nobody was helping me wake him up. "Someone. Anyone. Do something!" I looked over my shoulder, and they were all standing there, staring at my David.

That's when I saw the wound in his chest. The heavy headed axe had torn through flesh and bone. I could see his organs glistening wetly through the gaping wound, and blood was pouring from everywhere. The twins growled softly behind me in anguish.

"David, you're going to be fine! Stay with me!" I grabbed the wound and closed it, blood staining my white skin. "Somebody get a doctor. David? Can you breathe?"

"Kaede," Rome's voice said softly. He knelt on the ground beside me and put a hand on my shoulder.

"He'll be fine. Right? Werewolves can only die from silver bullets. I saw that in a movie."

"It was a movie, Kaede. In his wolf form, he might have withstood a blow like that, but…"

"Then make him shift. You're his alpha. Command him."

"Kaede-*sama*." Roki squatted down next to us, keeping his knees out of the ever-expanding pool of blood. "He is gone." I knew he was serious when I saw the tears streaming down his face.

He tried to pull me into a hug. Pushing him away, I snarled. "No! He can't be. He's not. Rome, make him better."

When the tears slid down his cheeks, I groaned in pain. Rome tilted his head and swallowed, trying to say something several times before he finally managed a weak, "I'm sorry, Kaede."

The scream that tore from my throat made everyone around me cover their ears. It didn't stop, and I wouldn't let it until the fucking gods, wherever they were, heard my anguish. The last little bubble of sanity inside me snapped like the inside of a glowstick.

From my knees, I jumped and landed on my feet. Spinning, I struck before anybody could stop me, shoving thick, daggerlike claws into Sabine's soft, exposed throat. Hot blood splattered my face, and I growled at her, fist tightening around the thick, sinewy insides of her throat. She gurgled and sputtered once before my fist blocked any chance of air escaping.

I pulled her face close to mine and locked my eyes with hers. My throat screamed in pain as I shouted a stream of obscenities at her, telling her I would see her in the darkest pits of Hell as I watched the light leave her eyes.

Until she was as dead as my David.

Yanking my hand from her throat, I turned around and walked away.

Chapter 16

How long I walked, I don't know. Probably not nearly as long as I lay in the snowbank, staring up at the clouds. My back was frozen when Roki found me. His face blocked my view of the fluffy cumulus clouds, and he was shouting my name, but I couldn't hear him. The whole world had been enshrouded in silence.

I closed my eyes when my face pressed against Roki's chest, and I fell asleep with the rhythmic pumping feeling from him running as he carried me back. There was a brief flash of the bathroom as he stripped me and got me into the shower. The next time I opened my eyes, I was lying in bed. The reality of what happened came crashing back, and I screamed before rolling back over and crying myself to sleep again.

Wake up, Little Wolf.

I'm a fox. I think.

Foxes don't have claws that can rend the flesh of their enemies. You should have used your teeth and tore the flesh from her neck and drank her blood.

Ewww. I focused on the blackness of my closed eyes. *Fenrir?*

Yes, Little Wolf?

David's dead.

Fenrir's touch, even just mental, had always been cool. This time he enrobed me in a warm blanket and whispered, *I know. I am sorry, Little Wolf.*

Why did he have to die?

To save you. He gave his life to keep you safe. He died happy knowing you would live. They probably sing songs of his deeds in the feasting halls of Valhalla as we speak.

You didn't make him jump in front of that blade, did you? To save me?

No. You did. He loved you with everything he was. When he saw your end, he did the only thing he could to save you.

I don't want to live, Fenrir. The anguish was back. Just when I thought I was getting better, with so much to live for. It had all been swept away with a single blow of an axe. I was tired. Sooo tired, and I just didn't want to go on anymore. *I'm tired of being a puppet.*

Cut your strings.

You said Gleipnir was unbreakable.

Cut your strings, not that which gives you power. You will need that.

For what?

To exact your revenge.

Sabine is dead, Fenrir. Revenge exacted.

Sabine was just another puppet. Would you seek vengeance against her or the puppeteer?

Hel's face invaded the blackness, chuckling merrily. Smashing it with a mental fist, I snarled. Freya's worried looking visage frowned at me. Another swipe of imaginary claws, and she was gone. I doubted they were truly looking in on me. I was completely insane now and probably just imagining them.

You are far from insane.

I wasn't that far before David was killed. Think it pushed me over the edge.

The insane do not ponder their condition. That alone should tell you something.

Potato, tomahto.

He chuckled. *The gods are too old for this world, Little Wolf. Would you help me free you?*

If I released him, they would pay. That much was for certain. He would devour them all. *Free me by freeing you?*

Free you by freeing everybody. If it were not for the gods' meddling, your David would still be with you.

Don't. Don't use him as bait to lure me into your trap. If I free you, it will be by my own will.

And your desire for vengeance.

That, too.

Little Wolf?

What?

I am sorry for your loss. Truly.

The warmth he had wrapped me in tightened a little. It felt almost like a hug. *Thank you. Fenrir?*

Yes?

What am I going to do? I don't know if I'm strong enough to go on, let alone face everything.

Those who are strongest do not see themselves that way. When you need it, your strength will be there. Now wake up, Little Wolf. Live.

Don't wanna.

But I was all bark and no bite. As soon as I said it, my eyes opened. Heat, not unlike Fenrir's, surrounded me. Blinking a couple of times, Remy's features, serene in sleep, came into focus. Lifting my head, I saw Rome behind me. At least I thought it was Rome, but without attitudes coloring their features, I wasn't certain.

My movement woke Remy. Romy. The one I was facing. "Hey." He rubbed his face and sat up, giving me a sad smile. "You alive?"

"Bad choice of words."

He frowned and nodded. "Sorry."

"He's really gone? It wasn't a horrid nightmare?" The tears started again. How I had any left, I don't know.

He sniffed and nodded sadly. "He's gone, Little Fox."

Rome. The tears intensified, and I peppered them with a few sobs. Rome lay back down and pulled me close, hugging me to his chest. "Shhh. He's probably hunting with his pack right now, missing the fuck out of you."

In shock, I pulled back. "Rome. I'm…" I didn't even know how to apologize to him for killing his sister. She was a twat, but she was still his sister, and I'd ripped her throat out. How the hell the two of them didn't hate me was beyond me.

"If you are going to apologize for what happened to Sabine, don't."

"I'm still sorry."

"Don't be. If you hadn't, I would have. She might be related to me by blood, but she was not my sister. David was more family than she. She lost that much the very first time she attacked you. I was the one who threw her in her prison cell, remember?"

I nodded and relaxed a little. He pulled me back to his chest. Against my better judgment, I pressed my forehead against him, letting him comfort me.

"She awake?" Remy lifted his head and looked over my shoulder.

"She is," I answered. "Where's Roki?"

There was a moment of silence between the two of them, and it worried me. I rolled back over so I could see both of their faces. "What?"

"He's talking to the headmaster."

Relief flooded me. I'd thought he'd been hurt. "Oh. What about?"

"Disenrolling you from the academy and taking you home…"

Judging from their faces, neither of them were too happy with his decision. I didn't know how to feel. Mostly, I was just shocked that he would do something like that without at least talking to me about it.

Then again, maybe he thinks I'm not capable of talking.

"Do you need anything?" Remy sat up.

"To pee. Do you still have those walkie-talkie stones?"

"Yes?" Rome looked at me curiously.

"Tell Roki to hold off. I need to think. Or try to anyway. No promises." I scooted to the end of the bed, almost having an accident. Lying flat, I hadn't noticed how full my bladder had been. I popped from the bed to the door, stepped outside, and popped to the end of the hall, bursting through the bathroom door. It would have sucked having to run that far.

As soon as my butt hit the too cold seat, "Kaede Tanaka, please report to the headmaster's office," boomed through the school.

"Not before I pee." I looked down at the light boxers and thin T-shirt I was wearing. "And get dressed."

Finishing up, I stopped at the sink long enough to splash my face with cold water and wash up a little. Thankfully, Roki had given me a shower to warm me up after my snow nap.

As soon as I looked at myself in the mirror, I started crying again. The pain of losing David reared its head for no reason whatsoever. I had a feeling it was going to be like that for a long, long time.

Sullen, I left the bathroom and took the time to walk back to my room. I needed a minute before facing anyone, especially the twins.

I'd left without my key, so I knocked on my own door.

"Thanks, Romy." I couldn't tell which one answered the door. They were just going to have to live with the moniker on the occasions I couldn't tell them apart.

"Rome."

"You guys need nametags."

"What fun would that be?"

He stopped chuckling when I glared at him. "I'm assuming you contacted Roki, and that's why I was summoned." I walked over to my dresser and pulled out a skirt, shirt, and undergarments and tossed them on my bed.

"Yes. He was surprised you were awake and informed the headmaster."

"Time to see what he wants."

"What *do you* want, Kaede?" Remy was still sitting on my bed. I could see him in the mirror on the dresser and could tell he wasn't excited about my answer.

"Honestly, I don't know. You two are literally the only two reasons I have to stay." *Unless you count my revenge.* I frowned at myself. If I were being honest, punishing the gods was more Fenrir's style. But there was still the matter of Steph. She was the one who had ended David's life. She was the one who did *everything* that Sabine said. If anybody deserved my revenge, it was her. *But is she worth sticking around for? I could go home, go back to my own life. Get drunk and dance with Hiroki. Try and forget David.* A sob escaped my lips, and I had to put my hands on my dresser to steady myself. Rome was there in an instant, holding me. I twisted in his grip and buried my face in his chest. "Don't suppose I could talk you guys into going to California?"

"I wish we could. Our contracts with the school are bound in blood, just as yours was. It would take a vote from the entire board of directors to nullify. *You* might get your wish after everything that has happened, but I'm afraid Remy and I are stuck here for quite some time."

Rome's heart beat a little faster. I could feel it against my forehead. "Would you want to go?"

"With you?"

190

I nodded against him, not daring to look up.

"Well, I can't let Remy have all the fun."

He made me smile. For the first time in over a day. "Thank you."

"You're very special to me, Little Fox. I'm sorry it took me so long to realize that."

I lifted my head and stood up on my tiptoes, kissing him on his chin. "Thanks."

He nodded and let go.

I lifted my shirt over my head and dropped my boxers. Rome's eyes bulged out of his head, he blushed, and turned around.

"What? You've seen me naked."

"Just wasn't expecting it."

"You can relax. I'm just getting dressed." I sighed and slipped on my panties and put my bra on. "There."

He turned around and stared as I stepped into my skirt and pulled it up over my hips. "You weren't dressed."

"Meh. The important stuff was covered. Figured you wouldn't mind seeing my…" I trailed off. The hurt of never getting to expose my panties to David another blow.

"Fox?"

I shook my head. "Sorry."

He nodded. "We miss him, too. He was pack."

"He was more than pack, he was our brother," Remy said solemnly. With all my aches and woes over losing my lover, they had to be feeling his loss just as bad as I. If not more.

I gave him a brief smile of understanding and pulled on my shirt, buttoning it up and looking around for my shoes. I saw the toe of one of them sticking out from under my bed. "Will you guys come with me?"

"You couldn't keep us away." The twin thing was cute, but it was kind of creepy when they said the same damn thing at the same damn time.

"Come in, Kaede."

I pushed the heavy door open the rest of the way and stepped into his office, Rome and Remy behind me. Roki was still there, I could see the top of his head over the tall-backed leather chair in front of Uncle Tatsuo's desk.

For the first time since I started school, Tatsuo decided I needed my uncle more than the headmaster. He stood up and walked around the desk, opening his arms to his niece.

Taking him up on his offer, I hugged my uncle and let him hold me. "I am so sorry for your loss, Kaede. David was a bright young man. He was good for you."

I nodded, having no doubt in my heart that I didn't deserve David. I'd just been lucky, damn lucky.

Uncle let me cry against him until I was ready to let go. When I finally did, he pulled me to the chair and helped me sit. "Your Hiroki and I were just discussing your enrollment at the school. I would like to hear your thoughts on the matter. Do you wish to go home?"

"Is it even an option?"

He returned to his seat, and I took the opportunity to shoot Roki an angry glare. He nodded once, realizing he had screwed up. It wasn't that I was opposed to the idea of going home, I was opposed to him discussing it without talking to me.

"Well," Uncle continued after he had settled in his almost throne-like chair, "There have been two deaths at the school. While that is not unheard of in past years, it certainly opens things up for review."

The reality of it hit me like a ton of bricks. There might be a chance I could go home, and the more I thought about it, the more I got excited about the prospect. But then I thought of Rome and Remy, and my heart sank into the pits of my stomach. Maybe lower. *Can I leave them? Can I forget about David, and them?* The answer was no. I would never forget any of them. Not even for a moment. *Could I still leave?* Maybe.

"Honestly, I don't know, Uncle. It might be safer with everything happening, but…"

"You would miss Hiroki and the Lateran brothers."

"Wait, what?"

"You would miss Hiroki and–"

"I freaking heard you. I'm asking what the hell you meant. You would send me home but not Hiroki? I'm the reason he's here in the first place!"

"It is not a question of what I would or wouldn't do. Decisions such as these are left to the board of directors. While they might be inclined to let *you* go, there is no chance for Mr. Nishimura to be released from his contract. We were discussing this before you joined us."

I looked at Roki, and he gave a slight nod.

"Then my answer is no."

"Kaede-*sama*…"

"Nope. No. *Non. Nein. Nō. Nei. Bangō.* Fuck that." The twins seemed a little disappointed that I would stay for Roki and not them, and I didn't blame them, but there was a *huge* difference in missing someone horribly, and not being able to live without him. Not to mention the fact that it was my fault he was there in the first place. He didn't fuck up and get sentenced to school, I did.

"Kaede-*sama*! It will be fine. You should go."

"No."

"He's right, Kaede." Remy agreed.

Rome was nodding.

Uncle Tatsuo was looking at me expectantly.

All that was missing was the Jeopardy Theme Song playing annoyingly in the background. "No. And you can't make me." I looked at my Uncle. "They can't, can they?"

193

He laughed and shook his head. "No, Kaede. They cannot make you. I do not know if it is even feasible or how the board would respond to such a request." He paused to think in his huge leather chair. He still managed to fill it, even in his human form. "Why don't we do this. Do not give me your answer now. *Think* about it. Discuss it with the boys. In the meantime, I shall present the *possibility* to the board members and gauge their reaction. Is this acceptable?"

I opened my mouth to answer, but Roki reached over and covered my mouth with his hand. "Yes."

Of course, I licked his palm. When he pulled it away after answering, I sighed and nodded. "Fine. I'm telling you I'm not going, but there is no harm in waiting to see what they say."

"Very good. *You*," he paused to point a long, slender finger at me, "are excused from classes for the remainder of the week. I shall let your instructors know."

"Thank you, Uncle."

He nodded. "You all are dismissed. Get some rest."

"Not much else to do with everyone else in class."

"Stay out of trouble, Kaede."

"Uncle, I'm too tired to get into trouble."

He nodded, but it didn't seem like he believed me very much.

Chapter 17

The last thing I was expecting was a soft knock on my door. Hiroki had left for class over an hour ago, and the rest of the students should have been studying hard to be good little humans, too. Ignoring it, I put my pillow over my head after burying my face into my mattress.

They knocked louder.

"Who is it?"

There was a muffled response that I couldn't make out, even with my supernatural hearing.

"Whoever it is, you suck dick." I growled and stood up, padding over to the door in my boxers and T-shirt. I wanted to give whoever it was a stern, disapproving look, but it was Fress and Kottr. "Ha! I was right."

"About?"

"Nothing. What do you want?"

"May we come in?"

Looking down at my attire, I almost said no, but they would probably be more interested in Roki wearing the outfit than me. "Sure."

Stepping back, I let them into my room.

"Sorry for the intrusion," Fress said meekly. I noticed when the two of them were together, he did most of the talking. It was a shame, because the timbre of Kottr's voice was much nicer. Not that there was anything wrong with Fress'.

"It's okay. I was just lying in bed. What can I do for you?" I motioned for them to sit on Roki's bed and sat on mine, propping myself against the headboard.

"We came for a few reasons. First and foremost, to apologize."

"For what?"

"Not being able to save your mate." Kottr finally spoke and then looked down at the floor, guilt weighing heavily on his face.

The familiar lump that appeared in my throat whenever I thought about David, or someone mentioned his name, made a reappearance. I swallowed before answering. "You had your hands full with Sabine. Sorry if I got any blood on you. And you have nothing to apologize for. I didn't know she had an accomplice with her, and neither did you."

"We are still sorry and can only imagine what you are going through. Is there anything we can do?"

"Not unless you can bring him back."

"Sadly, no. But we can bring you to him, if you would like to say goodbye? He is with our Mistress…"

I blinked in confusion. Their words not quite clicking in the old Kaede-brain. "I'm sorry. What?"

The looked at each other, silent communication passing between them before Fress got up and sat next to me on my bed. "Do you not remember your trip to Sessrumir? Where our Mistress gifted you with the *Seidr*? The day you became a *volva*."

"Did you just call me a pussy?"

He tilted his head in confusion. "*Volva*. Seer. Those gifted with fate magic."

"Oh. I thought you said vulva which is something *entirely* different. But yes? I do remember. When I died, I ended up in her hall… But I came back. Why can't David?"

The more I thought about it, the more excited I became and sat forward, practically ending up in Fress' lap.

He put a hand on my shoulder. "Because his body is dead. He died the moment the axe struck him, and no amount of magic could have kept him alive. You were stabbed. Your spirit was separated from your body in death, but the damage was not hopeless, and our Mistress used her magic to keep your body on the verge of death. He was…"

"Yeah. I was there. I saw." My heart broke again.

"But his spirit goes on to the next realm. Our Mistress is holding him for you…should you wish to say goodbye."

I wanted to scream, "Yes! Of fucking course, I do!" But my mind was blank, fear overwhelming me. I didn't know if I had it in me to talk to him again, to say goodbye. To be forced to spend another minute with him, and then have him ripped from me again. I wasn't that strong of a person.

"You do not." He wasn't asking, he was telling me. "I am sorry, I thought you would have wished time to tell him the things you did not have an opportunity to."

"It's not that."

"What is it, Kaede?" He tilted his head and ran the backs of his fingers over my cheek, wiping away the tears that I hadn't felt but should have expected.

"I'm afraid."

"Of him?"

"Of saying goodbye. Of losing my mind after going through losing him again."

"I understand. We are sorry to have asked."

"No!" I leaned forward and hugged him, grateful for their thoughtfulness. And of Freya's. I was being a moron. Again. If I *didn't* say goodbye, I'd regret it for the rest of my life, and I owed it to David. He loved me enough to lay down his life for me. "You are very kind. Yes. Please."

"Are you sure?"

"I was being a vulva."

He chuckled in understanding. "Are you ready?"

"As I'll ever be. Should I change?"

They both nodded, giving me strange smiles and standing. Fress reached out a hand and pulled me from the bed. Feeling something snap inside me, I looked around…and saw myself still sitting on the bed, a blank stare on my face. I reached out as my body toppled over sideways. I passed right through my hand and gave a muffled squeak.

"Be at ease, Kaede," Kottr rumbled, almost purring. "Not all of you may travel to Sessrumir."

Nodding in understanding, I had to ask, "How um…do we get there?"

They smiled and each took one of my hands, leading me out of my room, down the staircase, and outside. Just like before, even standing outside in nothing but my sleepwear, I wasn't the least bit cold. Nor did my breath fog in the morning sun. We had made our way outside in the middle of the break between classes, but nobody even looked at us. One student even walked *through* us.

I shuddered as a chill ran through me. "At least buy me dinner first, jerk!"

He couldn't hear us, either. Thankfully.

Fress hissed with laughter and let go of my hand, dropping to the ground on all fours and shifting into the same bluish hued mountain cat I'd seen before. Kottr shifted into his gray and a golden chariot materialized behind them, magically tethering itself to them. They both looked over their shoulder, and it didn't take a cat whisperer to know they were telling me to get my ass in.

"Keep it under the speed limit. And does this thing have seatbelts? I almost fell out three–" I had to grab on to the front edge of the chariot as it surged forward.

At least in my non-corporeal form, I didn't have to worry about freezing to death riding in an uncovered chariot through the hills of Iceland in winter. Especially when the chariot left said Iceland and pointed upward into Icesky and then Icespace. Non-corporeal or not, I started shivering and it had absolutely nothing to do with the temperature. Or lack of oxygen.

We leveled out, and then our nose dropped. Against my better judgement, I looked over the edge of the chariot and gasped. There really was a rainbow fucking bridge and waterfalls, and castles, and gods. Oh, my. Like any puny, somewhat mortal, I hurled. Thankfully, no non-corporeal chicken spewed out. It was more like a ghostly dry heave, and I just closed my eyes until I felt the wheels hit solid ground. I hit solid chariot floor and hung on for dear afterlife as we bounced over ridges in the same well-trudged path I had followed on my previous trip.

"At least...I...have a...ride this time."

We skidded to a stop in front of the familiar golden doors. Fress looked over his shoulder at me expectantly. Sighing, I stepped off the back of the chariot and fought the urge to kiss the ground. Instead, thoughts of David flooded my heart, and I found myself running toward the doors. As if on cue, they opened and I didn't stop until I was inside.

"That may be the most exuberant entrance I have ever seen into my hall."

I froze, fear outweighing my excitement. Freya was above me again, and I felt the ethereal blood in my veins freeze. "Nobody has ever had a greater reason to enter," I said respectfully. "Thank you." Finally, I built up the courage to look up at her and smile.

"Do not thank me yet." She started down the staircase, her slippered footsteps sounding like muted thunder with every step.

I bowed my head as she approached and felt her long, slender fingers through my hair.

"No gift of this magnitude may come without a price, my child. You understand that, don't you?"

"Yes, Freya."

"Good. Come have some tea, and we shall discuss payment."

The thrill of seeing David almost vanished as apprehension and fear warred inside of me. She might have given me the power to change fates, but apparently not my own. I just wish I had learned to master whatever that power was before David died and became a bargaining chip.

As soon as we sat on her luxurious couches in the sitting room, the elf brought us more tea. The chill that had settled in my bones on the ride and intensified at Freya's bargain, became minutely more bearable with the first sip. "What do you want?"

Freya eyed the contents of her cup, slowly brought it to her nose, and inhaled before gradually taking a sip. She swirled the contents gently in her cup and set it back down. "I think you know."

"Find Fenrir and kill him?"

"Just your promise."

"Pardon?"

She crossed her legs elegantly and folded her hands over them. "I can hardly keep the spirit of your David in my hall for the time it would take you to complete such a monumental task. All I ask in return for a chance to say goodbye to your beloved is your *word* that you will work to this end."

She didn't say when...

"Immediately."

Fuck.

"Such vulgarity."

"Will you tell me where he is?"

She shrugged. "You know his spirit is bound in your world and where. His body resides in Helheim. Do you think any mortal or god knows where besides his jailor?"

I thought of Sabine. She was close enough to Hel, that she might have been of some use. *Before* I ripped her throat out. Hopefully she was even *closer* to Hel. *Maybe her mother. But nobody has seen Headmistress Lateran in over a month.*

"I doubt even they knew. Hel would not let such information out. She draws even more power from the body of her brother. It is the main reason she doesn't wish him released on the Aesir gods. She is Vanir. She could not care less."

For all her high and mighty attitude, she just doesn't want to lose her battery backup?

I could *feel* Freya rummaging through my mind for an explanation of what a battery backup was. She chuckled when she found it. "More of an amp, but battery backup works just as well."

"So, just to make sure I got this straight, I promise to set forth on a glorious mission to find Fenrir and kill him, and I get to see David?"

She nodded.

"Deal." I stuck out my hand and she looked at it like it was covered in bio matter. It might very well have been as I tried to think if I touched myself inappropriately since the last time I washed my hands...

"Very well," she answered and stood, ignoring the rest of her tea. "Follow me."

The elf bowed as she passed, and I thought she flashed me a sad look, but I wasn't sure.

We exited the room, and she led me up the stone staircase she had just come down, without the thunderous footy steps this time. She must have saved those for grand entrances only. When we reached the top of the flight, we turned, and I gasped. There was a literally endless hallway lined with doors on both sides.

"Woah. You should open a hotel."

"It is. Of sorts. The price for a night's stay is much greater than most would want to pay." She laughed at her own joke. I just gulped and silently agreed with her. "Don't dawdle."

I understood why when we took our first step. A thousand doors whisked by with just one step. From her pocket, she pulled out an amber key, and unlocked the door on her left. "Kaede…"

"Yes?"

"He may not be the same David you remember. The dead quickly lose their memories. If he is happy, I suggest you do not ruin that for him."

"I won't." I couldn't. Not to the man who had literally given me everything.

She nodded, sensing the truth. "Simply knock when you wish to leave."

"Thank you." The tears were already threatening to leak out. I was so fucked.

With a gentle push, the door creaked open, and Freya let me in, gently shutting and locking it.

The room itself was rather simple, but beautiful. A bed, a desk, a chair. Some writing implements. But the view… There was no door to the outside balcony, it was just open and afforded a grand view of all of Asgard off in the distance. David was standing on that balcony, taking in the sights.

"David?" I called his name softly, slowly walking toward him.

He turned and smiled. "Is it my time?"

I choked down the little sob and made my smile a little bigger. "Not yet. They said I could visit you before you go."

"Oh. That was nice of them. And you. I know you…"

"Yes."

"Kaede?"

The tears started pouring free. I nodded at him, giving him a genuine smile this time, happy he at least remembered my name. "Yep. That's me."

"You didn't say yerp." He chuckled and held out his arms.

We nearly fell over the stone railing as I flew into them. "David," was the only word I could coherently get out as I turned into a blubbering mess.

"Shhh. It's okay."

"No, it's not! I miss you."

He kissed the top of my head. "I've missed you more."

I sighed, melting into his embrace and pressing my face against his chest. "Freya let me say goodbye to you."

"I know. She told me you were coming. I told her not to let you."

"What? Why?"

"Because the price was too high. Stay away from Fenrir, Kaede. There is no way to kill him."

I decided at that moment to follow Freya's advice and keep David happy. Even if it meant lying to him. "I figured, or someone would have done it long ago. Don't worry. I'm…going back to California."

"Good. Is that where you're from?"

"Yes." I shouldn't have been surprised he had forgotten, but I was. "I need to say thank you."

"What for?"

"Saving my life. Even if it cost you your own."

"It did? I don't remember that."

"Do you remember school?"

"Vaguely. I remember you. And two guys who looked a lot alike. Twins? Maybe. And a guy who had similar features to you but was much darker."

"Roki."

"Yes! Roki." He smiled as he pulled me from his chest so he could see my face. "I am going to miss you. But promise me you will be happy. Don't worry too much about your...me." His face contorted, having difficulty remembering his own name.

"I won't, David," I answered, subtly reminding him.

He nodded, smiling. "I am happy. It is very peaceful here, and after this, I get to join my ancestors on a great hunt, and then I will be reborn."

"That's great." I forced another smile and wiped my tears. "I just wanted to say goodbye and tell you how much I fucking love you." There was no way to stop the sobs that came after that. He knew and wrapped his arms around me again.

"I love you, too, Kaede. It's funny. I have forgotten almost everything, but not you. I could never forget you. I think I'm going to take my memories of you into the next life with me. Every moment we spent together still burns strong in my heart. I will find you if you want me to."

He sounded hopeful, and I couldn't take that from him. "I can wait twenty years or so. I'd wait forever if I had to."

I felt him heave against me as he breathed a sigh of relief. "Well. I think it's time for me to go. Remember not to worry about me. Just know that I love you with everything...I used to be. And will be." He pulled me away again and gave me a weak smile.

All I could do was nod. I was on the verge of an epic breakdown, and he didn't deserve that. He seemed truly at peace, and I was good with that. It made it a little easier. My heart was just torn over everything we wouldn't get to do together.

"I will." I managed to stutter.

He reached out and caressed my cheek, leaned in, and kissed me gently. "I love you. So damn much."

"I'll love you forever."

"And a day?"

"And a night."

I stepped back and quivered a smile, my lip trembling as the tears refused to stop. "Goodbye, my David. I love you."

"Goodbye, my little vixen. Tell everybody I'll miss them, too. Leave out the part where I forgot their names." He winked and started to fade from view.

"David. Be happy. Wherever you are, whatever you do, whomever you become. Be *happy*. You deserve it so fucking much." My eyes closed, and the epic meltdown came. When his fingers ghostly slid across my cheek, and his lips planted one feather-light kiss on my lips, I dropped to the floor in agony. "I love you," I whispered one last time.

When I finally looked up, he was gone.

"And he shall be reborn not as a wolf, but as the king of the skies, and he shall fly free," I muttered to the empty room, shaking my head to clear the murky numbness that had enveloped it.

Getting to my feet was an arduous task, but I managed and shuffled across the room, knocking three times on the green wooden door.

Chapter 18

"Kaede-*sama*?"

I opened my eyes in my own room, in my own bed, with my own Roki kneeling at my side and gently stroking my head. "Roke?"

"*Hai.* How are you feeling?"

"Better. David said to say goodbye."

"You were dreaming?"

I almost blabbed but decided against it. Visiting Asgard, saying goodbye to my lover, and promising to kill a god probably wasn't something he wanted or needed to hear. "Yes."

"Good. If you talk to him again, tell him I will miss him." He gave me a sad smile.

"I won't see him again, but if I do, I will."

"Do you wish to get some dinner?"

I almost said no, but then my stomach wailed the song of its people. "Uh. Sure. I could go for a little snack."

"Or twelve."

"Fine. I'm hungry."

He chuckled and stood, offering me his hand. "Kaede-*sama*?"

"Yes?" I took his hand and turned to the side of the bed, letting my feet touch the floor. He squatted in front of me, low enough to see into my eyes. "Are you going to be okay? Should I be worried? I know how much he meant to you."

I kissed Roki on the tip of his nose. "You know me."

"That is what I am afraid of. I looked around to see how many bottles of alcohol you consumed today and found none. That is when the worry started."

I stared at him in shock. Drinking hadn't even crossed my mind. "Yeah. That is weird. Now I'm worried about me, too."

He chuckled. "That sets me at ease." He stood and helped me stand up. "Come. They will start serving dinner shortly, and Rome and Remy-*san* are meeting us."

"Don't know how great of company I'll be…"

"Just being there is enough. There is no one else I would rather spend time with."

"Oh, Roki." I hugged him and sniffled. "Quit being so damn sweet. I'm tired of crying."

"I imagine you are. Just as I am surprised you have any left."

"My head is mostly liquid. Probably have a few buckets left."

"Huh." He gave me a confused look.

"What?"

"I thought it as mostly air…"

I laughed and slapped his chest, pulling my shirt over my head as I walked to the dresser. Roki snuck up behind me and put his arms around me, burying his face in my neck and inhaling deeply. "With everything that has happened. Should you need to talk…" He trailed off.

I patted his arm. "If I do, you will be the first to know."

"Promise?"

"I promise."

He let me go, letting his fingers slide over my naked tummy. There wasn't anything sexual about it, simply him trying to comfort me. He was staring at me in the mirror over my dresser and giving me a sad smile.

"What?"

208

"You have not been stuffing yourself the past few days. You need to eat more."

He was right. My cheeks were becoming a bit gaunt, and it really *hadn't* been that long since I'd eaten. I burned calories like rocket fuel. Nodding at him, I decided to double down. "Eight fried chickens and two Cokes."

"You would split wide open and waste all that food."

"Okay. Five fried chickens and a Coke. But I get dessert, too."

"Cheesecake?"

Nodding, I smiled at him, grateful for just the bit of normalcy he had given back to me with our silly conversations. He ran his fingers up my sides, and I squealed. "There is no tickling!"

"Then you should get dressed. I am finding it difficult not to touch you."

I nodded. "Sorry."

"I know you are far from the mood. Do not worry. I shall behave. But do me the favor of *never* apologizing for exposing any amount of your flesh. It is far from a hardship to gaze upon you."

"You like seeing me naked?"

"There is not a man on this earth who would not. You are not eye candy; you are a feast."

"You say the sweetest things to me. Thank you."

He blinked at me over my shoulder in the mirror, surprise and worry coloring his face. "*Hai*."

"Quit worrying. I'm okay. Just extra mushy today."

"Your head or your heart?"

"Bit a both." I chuckled and pulled my bra on.

"Allow me?"

"Yep."

He settled the straps over my back and hooked them for me before sliding his hands around and tugging the front down just a hair. "Perfect."

I slipped my shirt on and Roki reached around and buttoned it for me.

Pulling out a pair of panties, he turned me and knelt down, sliding my boxers off and then holding out my underwear for me to step into. I giggled as his fingers slid over my hips. He was being a perfect gentleman and not staring, but I still felt myself getting a little turned on by the intimacy of the situation.

"Skirt?"

I handed it to him, and he held it out for me. I stepped into the circle of blue fabric. He pulled it up over my legs as he stood, tucked my shirt in and zippered it up.

"Thank you, Roki."

"My pleasure."

I put my socks and shoes on myself and grabbed my blazer from the closet, twirling it around me as we headed for the door. We held hands as we walked to the Dining Hall, and for the first time in days, I relaxed, even if only marginally. Saying goodbye to David had hurt, but it had also healed me somewhat. I wasn't a blubbering mess, but I definitely wasn't myself.

Who I was exactly, remained to be seen.

Roki looked around for the twins as soon as we entered.

"They shall show up as we pile our plates high."

"Pardon?"

I shook my head, clearing the somewhat familiar feeling. "Nothing."

He gave me a quizzical look but didn't say anything as we got in line for food. I was in the mood for beef instead of chicken, practically salivating at the pile of steaks in the silver serving tray. I took three of them and two baked potatoes. Some meatloaf, green beans, a bit of pot roast. Some sliced roast beef and a hamburger. The hamburger had just rolled off my plate and onto my tray, when the twins crept up behind us.

"Holy shit. I see your appetite is back."

It was Rome. Remy was smarter than that. "Hi, Rome."

"Remy."

Okay then, maybe not. "I said Remy."

"Uh huh. How you doing?"

I set my tray down on the rails in front of the buffet and turned around. The three of them stared at me. "New rule. Nobody is allowed to ask Kaede how she is doing. Okay? I'm managing, not great, but not bad, either. I don't expect it to change within the next year. So, please… Do not let that question leave your lips again."

"*Hai.*"

"Sorry," the twins mumbled in unison.

"Don't be. I know you're just worried about me." I turned around, picked up my tray, and headed for the desserts. Two slices of cheesecake, and I was heading for the drinks.

"You have your hands full. You want a Coke?"

I nodded. "Thanks, Remy."

"Rome."

"Whatever." I headed for our normal six-top table and stopped dead in my tracks. My heart heaved, and I closed my eyes, sighed, and turned away. I chose a new table for just the four of us, in a section we had never sat in before. There were far fewer memories, and it was nowhere near the spot David had died.

I sat and let the tears fall, getting them out of my system before the guys got to the table. When I saw Roki out of the corner of my eye, I wiped them away and dug into my food. "Mmm. Food."

"Hai." His tray settled down next to mine, and he sat, his hand patting my knee gently. As far as acting went, I

was pretty damn good. It would be a cold day in Helheim before I ever pulled one over on Roki.

"I couldn't even walk over there."

"I found it difficult and unnerving as well. You cannot even tell there was a... What happened."

"Bleach."

"Hai." He nodded and slipped a forkful of rice into his mouth, chewing quietly.

I couldn't even look over there. Luckily Rome and Remy sat down in front of me, effectively blocking my view of that half of the dining area. And most of the southern hemisphere. The Lateran Wall.

Rome shifted a Coke from his tray to mine and slipped me a smile. "Your drink, madam."

"Thank you, kind sir. Such a gentleman."

"I try."

"Sometimes," I said with a little wink. I *really* didn't want to start a fight.

A presence slipped into my mind, quietly observing. I knew it was Fenrir. He had a certain *feel* that I usually only noticed when we were conversing. For me to notice it when we weren't was new.

Can I get you something?

He seemed a little startled that I noticed him and was silent for a moment. *Where were you?*

Pardon?

Earlier today, I tried to find you and could not. Where were you?

Uncle Tatsuo wanted me to get some rest after everything that happened. He put me in the infirmary under a shield so nobody would bother me. By nobody, I mean you.

His wolfish chuckle rattled my teeth, but he believed my lie. *Tell the dragon not to hide you from me again. I do not like worrying about you.*

212

Awwww. You were worried about me? You're so sweet. And you tell the dragon that. He might char my ass.

It would be the last thing he did.

You like my little butt, don't cha.

It is pleasing, yes. You seem to be in better spirits.

The rest did me some good. And the elven nurse gave me some happy pills.

I understand. Time grows short, Little Wolf. It is near the time for you to find me. Enjoy your meal...and the company.

Night, Fenrir.

He slipped from my mind, and I came to with all three of my dinner dates staring at me intently. "What?"

"Did he leave?" Rome looked around the room after he asked.

"Yerp. Went night-night."

"Thankfully."

"Something is weird, though."

"What?" Remy leaned forward.

"I can lie to him now. I could *never* do that before. Not to a god. They always saw right through it."

"They?" All three of them asked simultaneously.

"Yes? Hel and Fenrir."

"Kaede-*sama*. What *aren't* you telling us?"

Okay, maybe Roki wasn't the *only* one who could see through my bullshit. I set my fork down and debated spilling my guts, but fear of Fenrir overhearing our conversation got the better of me. I mouthed the word, *later*, and tapped my ear.

They nodded in understanding.

Kaede Tanaka, please report to the headmaster's office.

"Oh, come the fuck on!" I pointed at my food with both hands.

"Eat," Rome said simply and pulled one of the stones out of his pocket. He closed his eyes for a moment, then returned the stone to his pocket.

"Wert da ferk?"

"The walkie talkie stones, as you called them."

"They're telepathic?"

He and Remy nodded.

"That's fucking *cool*. Where's mine?"

"You don't get one," Rome said and took a bite off his chicken leg.

"Why?"

"Because you would overload the circuits with your constant prattle." He winked, just as I had a moment before.

"Okay. I can see that." I cut a piece of steak off and groaned as I put it in my mouth. "Vats fuffin gvood."

"Don't talk with your mouth full."

"You've never seen me with my mouth full. Your brother has, though." I wiggled my eyebrows. Totally worth it to see Rome blush through the red spectrum.

Remy laughed at his brother's discomfort. "She's not lying."

"Knock it off," Rome whispered.

"Aww. You jealous, Rome?" I grinned at him and took another bite.

"Maybe."

It was no fun teasing him when he was being honest like that. I sighed and chewed, savoring the taste of the steak. Until I saw Roki staring at me. "What?"

"I could not help but notice your plate. You are hopelessly addicted to chicken and fish. Why the dietary change?"

"I was craving meat?"

Rome and Remy both snickered.

"Shut up. You know what I meant." I looked back at Roki, who had one eyebrow cocked. "What? You've seen me devour meat before." There were more snickers, but I ignored them.

"Yes, but I have *never* seen you eat nothing else."

"I put a vegetable, potatoes, and cheesecake on my tray."

"And yet they all remain untouched…"

I looked at my plate, and he was right. I had eaten two of my four steaks, and the rest of the beef on my plate without noticing. Probably when I was conversing with Fenrir. Nor had I noticed when I pointed at my plate when the announcement came to go see my uncle. The rest of the food sat untouched. "Huh. Must be low on iron or some shit." I unwrapped the potato and took a bite. "Fee? Pvotafo."

He shook his head and continued eating his own food.

"If hvot." I waved my hand in front of my mouth, trying to cool it off and opting to take a sip of Coke, letting the scalding tuber cool in a bath before swallowing.

∞ ∞ ∞

"Hello, Kaede. Gentlemen, I do not recall summoning you to my office…"

"I asked them. Whatever you want to yell at me for, I don't care if they hear, and I have something to tell them, and I need you to help."

"I did not call you here to berate you. I just like summoning students without entourages." He sighed and backed away from the door, letting us pile in his office.

"What did you need, Uncle?"

"Headmaster."

"Sorry, what did you need, Uncle Headmaster." I figured a little light banter would lighten the mood he was

215

obviously in. His scowl told me I might have been a little wrong.

"First, tell me why you need me to help you talk to the men who have absolutely no difficulty understanding your gibberish?"

I made a dome motion with my hands and wiggled my fingers at the wall.

He narrowed his eyes, but obviously sucked at charades.

I had a flash of inspiration. "Have you ever seen Star Trek?"

"Yes?"

"What is the first thing they put up when the Klingons are circling their anus?"

"The joke is *Uranus*."

I growled in frustration. "The anus isn't important!" There was a chorus of muffled laughter behind me. "The answer was *shields*." I motioned frantically at the walls.

"Shields? You wish me to shield the office?"

I slapped my forehead.

"Yes, Headmaster-*dono*. She does not wish to be overheard."

He nodded and lifted his hands. We all stuck our fingers in our ears and wiggled them as the shield slammed into place with a *thud* of displacement.

"Is that better?" He turned and walked to his desk, motioning to the chairs in front of it, not that there were enough for all of us. Instead of sitting he stood beside his chair, which was swiveled and facing the window behind his desk. I didn't think anything of it until it turned around, and I saw Freya sitting in it.

I dropped to the chair I'd been about to sit in, in complete shock. "Freya…"

"I see you have met," Uncle said unsurprisingly. "May I introduce you to the chairman, chairwoman in this case, of Aesir Academy."

"Hello, Kaede."

The guys took a knee, Roki included.

"Rise. We don't do that here."

They did, visibly shaken by our distinguished visitor.

"I assume you were going to tell everyone about your visit this morning and wished for one of your Uncle's fabulous shields, so you would not be heard by wolfish ears?"

I nodded, still in shock. Unsure if she was pissed that I was going to blab, I just couldn't handle the secrets anymore. Not from Roki, especially. He was starting to see through them.

"You may."

"Wait, *you're* the Chairman of the Board?"

"Yes. And your request to leave Aesir Academy has been summarily dismissed. I assume you do not have a question as to why?"

"No, ma'am."

"Good."

"Wait…" Rome protested, and Uncle Tatsuo shot him a look that would have silenced a charging army. Not Rome, though. Nope. "If she goes home, Fenrir loses his herald. He won't wake up, and everybody will be safe."

"If Kaede leaves, he will simply find another herald," Freya said coolly.

Rome felt the frigid bite in her response and shut up.

"Then how are we going to keep her safe?"

Freya stood. "That is simple. She and I have devised a plan that will solve everyone's problem."

"What is that?" Uncle Tatsuo had apparently not been made aware of the plan.

"She's going to kill Fenrir."

Chapter 19

The silence in the room was deafening. The looks the four men were giving the goddess were unpleasant. And the beating of my heart was reaching hummingbird proportions.

"You expect my niece to kill…a god?"

"Sure. Mortals killed gods all the time back in the old days. They just need the right weapon!"

The looks she was getting weren't any better. At least Uncle had asked the question I'd been too afraid to ask. "The gods themselves couldn't slay him! At best, all they could do was subdue him, split his soul and body, and bind him! How in Helheim do you think this scatterbrain, no offense my niece, is going to kill him?"

"None taken, Uncle." I knew it, and up until lately, had been proud of the fact.

"What has changed?" Tatsuo crossed his arms over his chest, practically glaring at the formidable god before him.

She smiled, almost evilly. "He has shared his bonds with her. They are becoming one."

"The tattoos? Gleipnir?"

"More than that. Have you seen her vixen as of late?"

"What?"

She turned to me. "Show him, my dear. Show him your fox."

The color drained from my face. The only one who knew was Fenrir and Lornca…

"That is right, Kaede. Lornca's mate is the one who served you tea." She grinned proudly like she had outsmarted a teenage deviant at her own game.

"Kaede?" Tatsuo asked concernedly.

I sighed and shifted. *Might as well get it* all *out in the open.*

There was a collective gasp as my newly acquired fox-wolf hybrid form came into view. I circled, slowly chasing my own tails so everyone could get the whole effect.

"Kaede-*sama*?"

I gave Roki a sad look, as effectively as I could in my new form, and lowered my eyes in apology. Unable to stand the looks I was getting, I shifted back.

"Well, that was unexpected."

I turned to Roki, and he winked at me. He had seen it before but had the tact not to mention it. I should have known better. "You still love me, even if I'm a little husky?"

"Still beautiful."

"And deadly," Freya chimed in. "If anybody can kill him, it is she."

"With what weapon? No blade forged in Asgard, Migard, or any of the nine realms may harm him!"

Freya sat back down in Tatsuo's chair. "There are other realms. Midgard seems to be the constant in all of them, a realm of many beliefs, gods, and pantheons. She, herself, has only just stepped into ours. She's had a weapon forged in none of the nine realms at her disposal all her life…"

"My katana." They were gifts from the Inari-*kami*. The Japanese god of agriculture, wine, *and* blacksmithing. They were forged in his hearths in the heavens and stayed there until we called for them. It was a gift to all *kitsune, nogitsune,* and *inari foxes*. It was the one remaining thing I still possessed from the Inari-*kami*.

I missed *sake*.

Closing my eyes, I called my blade and didn't even need to look to see if it was there. I could feel it humming in my hand. Holding it out before me, I opened my eyes.

"It is too dangerous," Tatsuo said calmly. "He will sense her intent and end her life before she even gets close to him."

"His body is bound by Gleipnir and hidden by Hel herself so she can bolster her powers with his. It is not Fenrir that you need to worry about, it is her. She will not give his body up easily."

"I still say it is too dangerous."

"Good thing it is not your call, child of Jormungandr."

Tatsuo let out a hissing breath and nodded. "Fine, but if she is not up to the task, we will not force her."

"But she has already given me her oath."

"What?"

Freya smiled and looked at me. "Isn't that right, child?"

Ruh-roh. "Um…about that. She's right, Uncle."

"What? How? When?"

It was Rome who answered. "While we were in class, and she was alone. She went to say goodbye to David. I smelled him on her at dinner and thought she hugged a jacket of his, or something. But I also smelled two kitties on her. Now it makes a little more sense."

I blushed and nodded.

"So, when you told me David said goodbye to all of us…"

"He really did. I just didn't think you'd believe me."

Roki smiled.

My uncle called a chair into being, how I didn't have a clue. One second it wasn't there, the next it was as he sat down on it. "Kaede…"

"I know. I screwed up. Shocker, right?"

"No. You did not. You were coerced by gods into this little play. I just wish it had been someone else."

221

"More capable?"

He shook his head. "With a different mother. She is absolutely going to take my tail, if not my head, for this."

"Too bad you only have the one, huh?" I flared my nine behind me and grinned at him.

"Little shit."

"Learned it from my uncle."

∞ ∞ ∞

"Anybody else having serious déjà vu right now?"

"With the volcano, yes. The ride, not so much," Rome shouted over the wind. "I would have preferred riding in one of the charons' cabs…"

I had to agree with him. Freezing my little foxy ass off while riding a chariot through the skies of Iceland on my way to Hell wasn't exactly traveling in style. But when a god offers you their personal mode of transportation, refusing is not an option.

I was pretty sure Fress and Kottr heard our conversation. They gave us disdainful looks over their harnessed shoulders.

"No offense!"

They sloped down, and I nearly fell out of the chariot. Inertia was not my friend. Before we left, Uncle Tatsuo had given me a thirty-pound necklace, carved from bone, and covered in draconic runes. I was pretty sure it had been carved *for* a dragon. It was that big. I looked like Flavor Flav. *But* it was like a portable shield generator. When I pressed a series of the runes, it turned on or off, casting a shield much like the one Tatsuo could cast. It would at least keep Fenrir from knowing what we were up to, and hopefully stop Hel from realizing we were taking a stroll through her back yard.

As for finding Fenrir's body, Tatsuo had told me to, "Follow my heart." Whatever that meant. Freya didn't seem too worried about me finding him, either.

I looked around the larger than normal chariot at Rome, Remy, and Roki. Pain gripped my heart. David's absence was something we were all ignoring and finding it impossible to ignore at the same time. We all felt it. Nobody talked about it. Geri was missing, too, but neither Tatsuo or Freya trusted her to go with us. She was a child of Fenrir *and* bound to him and me through Gleipnir. He might feel her presence even through the draconic shield.

As the chariot passed through the cave on the side of the volcano, we all instinctively ducked. There was plenty of room, but nobody wanted to get decapitated by a stalactite. When the cave opened up into a large cavern, Fress and Kottr set the chariot down on the hard-packed earth. As soon as we filed out, they shifted, and the chariot disappeared

"Where to?" Fress asked while I looked around in wonder.

The cave opened in two directions. The one leading south led to the city of the dead, home of Hel. I pointed in the opposite direction and answered, "That way," and took off at a brisk pace, wanting to put as much distance as possible between me and all the dead souls that could burn your flesh with just their touch.

"Do you feel Fenrir?" Roki fell into step next to me.

"No. I feel a hankering not to be surrounded by dead people."

"A wise choice, unless the god we seek is, in fact, in the city of the dead…"

Damn him and his logic. Closing my eyes, I felt around to see if anything seemed out of the ordinary. It took all of a second to realize I wasn't going to feel *shit* on the inside of a magic bubble. "Uhh… Can't feel anything with this necklace. And I'm not shutting it off until we are safely back at the school. Or Fenrir is dead."

"So, we are to stumble around blindly?"

"I guess."

"That seems a better choice than broadcasting our location to the gods."

I nodded at Hiroki. "Glad you agree."

"Might I make a third suggestion?"

"You know, you might have led with that and saved us some time bantering."

"I enjoy your witty responses."

"What is your suggestion, Roki?"

He smiled and shifted, scenting the air with his delicate fox nose.

"Show off."

He winked and led the way. I debated shifting, too, but Roki's nose was a hundred times stronger than mine. He spent much more time in his fox form than I did, but I wasn't sure if it was that, or just his physically enhanced body that made it that way. I sucked at everything, even being a fox.

He rounded a bend in the cave, and I worried until we caught up, but he was waiting there for us. "I smell decay," he whispered through his muzzle.

"More dead people."

He nodded.

"Guards," I whispered over my shoulder and felt a ripple as the twins shifted into their hellhound forms. They shouldered me aside and took the lead.

Fress and Kottr surrounded me, letting just their hands shift and extending their claws. "Stay between us," Kottr rumbled.

There was a brief clash of metal against metal, and the crunching of bone. Rome and Remy made an effective wall, and I couldn't see what they had come across until they spread out in a hollowed-out section of cave, a narrow doorway on the other side. The six skeletal guards were strewn about the room.

"I…fall to pieces," I sang as we passed through. Everyone turned and shot me a warning glare. "What? They can't hear."

The Romies shook their heads. Even in hound form, I couldn't tell them apart by looking at them. They shifted back quickly, unable to fit through the doorway with their massive frames. Even in their human forms, it was a tight fit. Luckily, the corridor wasn't very long, and my claustrophobia didn't have a chance to kick in.

We stepped out onto another balcony with stairs on both sides, leading down to…the city of the dead. For a brief moment, I *hoped* it was a *different* city of the dead, but the half-destroyed center where Hel had clawed her way through was only moderately repaired. Their public works department left a lot to be desired. The northern passage led to the same damn place, just a different way.

"Fuck me." I leaned over the natural stone ledge to get a better view.

"You have a horrible sense of propriety and place," Rome chuckled.

"Huh?"

"You said… And then you bent over the… Never mind."

"Did you just make a dirty joke at a time like this?"

"I'm sorry."

"Don't be. I'm proud of you." I grinned at him. "Wait. You're Rome, right?"

"Yeees?"

"Just making sure."

He rolled his eyes and shook his head. "What now, fearless leader?"

"Guess we're going to town."

"Maybe not…"

I turned to Roki, who had shifted to see over the ledge a little better. "What?"

"Just looking at the destroyed portion of the town."

"Yes?"

"Hel came at us from underneath the city of the dead…yes?"

"Yes."

"That would suggest that there is more to Helheim *beneath*."

"You think she has him chained up in the basement?"

"*Hai*."

"Makes sense to me, but we're still going to have to go *into* the town to go down."

"Perhaps not," he said and motioned me closer. When I was standing next to him, he pointed at the outer walls behind the city, a part we would not have been able to see had we taken the southern branch of the cave system. We would have come out overlooking the front. By taking the northern passage, we were looking at the city from the side. "See the passages along the wall behind the city?" He pointed off to our right where the cave wall and floor met. Barely visible, three stone doors were nestled closely opposite a gate in the city wall.

"Huh. Told you we were going the right way."

"Yes. You are brilliant. Think we can get to those doors without being seen?"

"Well, the dead aren't the most observant of people, but maybe we should shift and split up. A few strays would be even *less* noticeable than six people walking through a vast open cavern."

"As I said. You are brilliant."

"What about this, though?" I fingered the heavy necklace around my neck.

"Might make a good doggie collar," Roki said with a hissing chuckle.

"Fuck off, fox," Rome said grumpily.

"He's right, though," I answered thoughtfully and walked up to Rome. "Rome, would you shift and carry this big heavy collar for little old me?" I ran my finger down his chest and gave him a sultry smile.

"Well. Er…uh."

"So articulate when you're flustered."

He sighed and nodded. "I would love to."

"Thank you, Romeo."

"No. Never call me that."

"You don't want me to be your Juliet?"

"Since they both died at the end, no. I don't."

"Good point," I said, straightening and taking on a more serious demeanor. "Shift, and I'll put it on you. I want to get it from my neck to yours as quickly as possible. Not entirely sure how this thing works, and I think the fastest we get it from me to you, the less chance of it shutting off."

He nodded and stepped back, shifting right in front of me. Magic washed over my skin as he did, sending goosebumps up my arms.

"Ready?"

His head bobbed once, and I lifted the necklace over my head and slid it over his, having to hold down his ears to get it over and onto his neck. The medallion settled against his massive chest. "Good doggie."

His tongue, nearly as wide as my head, shot out and swiped across my face. I shot him a horrified look as doggie drool dripped from my chin. "Oh, my fucking gods. That was disgusting. Bad doggy!" I bopped his nose.

He sneezed and let out a doggie chuckle.

"Laugh it up, furball. The odds of you licking me ever again just went down exponentially."

He gave me puppy dog eyes and whined a little.

227

"We all need to stay within thirty feet of him for the necklace to cover us. Kitties, keep close. Roki, shift and ride Remy."

He nodded, seeming a little more excited than he should. "You are going to ride Rome-*sama*?"

"Yerp."

"Congratulations," he said to the shifted Rome and gave him a little wink. Everyone else shifted and took their positions.

I shifted into my hybrid form and ran up Rome's leg, settling myself on his neck behind his massive head. "Let's go," I said with a little more difficulty than usual into Rome's ear. He nodded and took off at a slower than normal pace, sticking to the shadows where his black fur blended in. If it weren't for the white-gray blob on his back, he would have been totally undetectable.

I turned my head and saw Remy right on his tail. Literally. The black and blue cats were weaving through his moving legs as we walked. Hopefully, by the grace of *kami*, we would make it to the three doors without a horde of angry skeletons and zombies after our heads.

We almost made it, too.

Halfway to the doors, the gates in the wall opened, and skeletons poured out by the droves. They didn't frighten me as much as the detachment of angry looking spirits that followed them, the ones that burned your flesh if they touched you.

"You see them?" I hissed at Rome. He was touching me, and out of all of them, had the best chance at seeing them.

His head bounced as he slammed on his doggie brakes. I slid over his shoulders onto the ground in front of me. With his massive nose, he pushed me toward the doors and bounded off at the army of undead.

"Fool," I hissed, but my heart swelled a little. He didn't need to beat them, just hold them off for a few minutes. His strides were over double of any of ours, except Remy's. He could catch up once we were through whichever door we picked.

The only problem was, he had the damn necklace. As he bounded on top of the first row of skeletons, I was sure that he had forgotten that little fact.

Taking our chances, I headed for the doors. Up close, they were much larger than I thought, and we were probably going to need both hellhounds to push them open. Without the necklace, something was pulling me toward the furthest door, and I made a beeline for it, as fast as my little legs could propel me.

Skidding to a stop, Roki leapt off Remy and shifted, hitting the ground and calling for his sword. The kitties chose to remain in their much deadlier panther-sized forms with wicked claws and teeth. Remy, too. But I could see him wanting to join his brother in the battle.

I shifted and whistled at Rome, "Come on, boy. Come here. You want to go for a ride?"

He looked over his shoulder and shot me a death glare, before swiping at another row of skeletons and then turning around. With a leap, he was away from the rest of the still standing skeletons, the specters closing in fast. He took off running toward us.

"How do we open this thing?" Roki sounded almost frantic.

I looked up and saw rungs about five feet above my head. There was no way to reach them without a ladder. Remy moved me out of the way, went up on his haunches, and gripped it with his teeth, pulling on it. It didn't budge.

"Should we try a different door?" Roki looked at the other two we had passed.

"No. This is the one. I'm sure of it. Remy, try pushing?"

He spit out the rung and hit the front door with his paws, with no effect whatsoever. They were barred or locked.

I looked around for a doorbell, something, anything. The specters were much faster than the skeletons and not far behind Rome. We were running out of time.

Out of desperation, I looked at the intricate carvings on the door, trying to make sense out of what I was seeing, but they blurred in my vision.

"Past the city where no living soul resides, lies the doors to Helheim. None shall enter without invitation, and only the servants of gods hold the crimson key."

"What?"

"What?" I was just as shocked as Roki, even though the words had come out of my mouth. "What the fuck does that mean? Why can't these stupid things be in fucking English?"

"This is the way. You are a servant of a god. Crimson key? Did anybody give you a key?"

"No!'

Fress shifted, rolled his eyes at me, and grabbed my wrist. One claw slid from the tip of his finger, and he poked me in the palm, blood swelling from the fresh wound. He placed my palm against the door. "Whenever crimson is mentioned in a vision, you can always bet it means blood."

The door clicked and opened, partially. "Oh. Thanks. And ouch."

He lifted my hand and ran his raspy tongue across the wound. It healed, and he gave me a wink. "Remy?"

The hellhound pushed the door open with his massive head. The five of us slipped through and held it open for

Rome to get inside. I started bouncing in fear. The specters were almost upon him, and it was going to be close…

"Hurry!"

"He is." Roki pulled me out of the way just as Rome leapt the remaining distance, landing on just this side of the threshold.

Remy started pushing the door closed, and we all fucking helped him. Spectral arms slid inside just as the door slammed shut. Luckily, the severed limbs evaporated into black mist instead of falling to the ground.

"That was close. Who's up for a nap?" I slid down to the ground and leaned back against the door. "Anybody bring anything to eat? I'm starving."

Roki pulled out a Powerbar from his pocket and dangled it in front of my face.

"Ew," I said with a look of utter distaste on my face as I reached out and took it. "These things are disgusting." I tore the package open and chomped off the corner, chewing loudly. "You couldn't *pay* me to eat one of these if it weren't an emergency."

"Sorry. Next time I shall bring *bento* boxes."

"Was that sarcasm? Cuz that wouldn't be a bad idea. I could really go for some *udon* and rolled-omelets. Oh! *Oumurice* would really hit the spot right now."

The shrieking of tortured souls ruined the rest of my appetite.

Chapter 20

It was cold outside. It was *colder* in Helheim. Funny me, you'd think Hell would literally be hot. Nope. My breath not only fogged, but crystalized mid-air, and I scratched an arm on my nipple.

"What the fuck?" Instead of shifting into my fox form, I opted for my demi-form, sighing in relief once I was ensconced in my nice, warm fur coat.

"Cheater." Rome stroked the hair on my face, creating a shiver that had nothing to do with the sub-arctic temperatures.

"Did you just pet me?"

He blinked in surprise. "I did. I'm sorry. Your fur just looked so soft…"

"Do it again," I said and leaned against him, grinning up and exposing teeth that were a little too sharp in my fur covered human face.

He blinked at the ears on top of my head. "You're adorable."

"Hehehe. Perv. Like the fox-girls, huh?"

"Uh… You're not that foxy. More wolfy."

"Shit. You forget about stuff like that when you can't see yourself." I pouted.

"Even wolfy, you're still a fox." He ran his fingers over my pelt again and smiled.

"Hellhounds don't have a demi-form?"

He shook his head. "All or nothing."

"What about kitties?" I asked before I turned around. Had I just looked, I would have had my answer. Fress and Kottr were still human, but furred. Cat ears stuck out above their heads. "Dawwwwwwww."

They blushed when I got gushy over their cuteness. Not as in red cheeks, but they lowered their faces and looked everywhere but at me.

"Focus, Kaede-*sama*." I gasped when I saw Roki. He was hot as a human. As a demi…. *Holy fuck.* His fur was thick and red, but white around his muzzle, down his neck, and I'm sure his belly. Maybe other places. *Might have to explore just how far later.*

I'd seen his demi-form before, but like most things about himself, he tended to keep it under wraps unless absolutely necessary to expose another side of himself. I could have counted the number of times I'd seen it before on two fingers. I was still staring when he put his fingers in front of my face and snapped.

I blinked. "What? You're hot. Sorry, not sorry."

He just shook his head and turned away, trying to see down the dark corridor leading away from the door. "You are sure this is the right way?"

"It's where my gut pointed me. If I was wrong, feel free to hate my guts."

"I do not think I could." He bowed.

"Stop being a suck. C'mon. Let's go kill a god." I stopped moving, and the hallway faded away. "Not all paths are straight. Not all intentions are pure. Trust not those who would have you seek death for it is of nefarious intent."

"What?" Hiroki grabbed my hands. "What did you say?"

"Beats the hell out of me. Something about crooked paths and not trusting people. I sound like a fucking fortune cookie."

"Kind of taste like one, too," Remy said as he walked past me, winking. I assumed he was Remy, since Rome had no idea what I tasted like. Except my face. Doggy drool. Yuck.

I started walking again, ignoring Roki's worried expression as I left him standing there trying to decipher my ominous prophecy. He caught up and whispered quietly. "Maybe it means we should not trust Freya?"

"She's like the god of gods. The big wig. Head honcho. Gots Odin's balls in her purse. If we can't trust her, then who can we trust?"

"Ourselves," he answered without hesitation.

"Well, I'm not going to start second guessing everything because of some super stupid power that *she* gave me. Why couldn't she give me something cool, like wings. Or telepathy. Or firebolts! I want firebolts. We could warm this place up."

"You *have* fire. You just refuse to learn to harness it."

"Uh. That's more my father's thing. I'll stick to being cute and eating a lot."

"Truly, you are unbeatable."

"If you're gonna be good at something, be good at what you love."

He snickered. Something dirty popped into his brain. I could always tell. "Perv."

"*Hai.*" He bumped my hip with his, and we slammed into the back of Rome and Remy, not having paid enough attention to the path ahead of us.

Rome flashed us an angry look and made a shushing motion with his finger. He moved away from Remy and let me through.

"Okay, wrong door," I whispered, praying to whatever god that would listen and not try to kill us that we could get out of Helheim without being seen by Hel *or* Headmistress Lateran. They were both in a cavern about a hundred feet down from the ledge where we stood. The path we were on wound around it several times before opening at the bottom.

"What the fuck?"

Rome clasped his hand over my mouth, even though I only whispered. He made a shushing motion again and pointed at his ear. I stared at him blankly.

He rolled his eyes and motioned at his brother. Remy walked forward, and Rome reached into his twin's blazer pocket and handed me one of the walkie talkie stones.

As soon as it touched my palm, I heard him. *Be quiet! My mother has better hearing than I do. If we're lucky, she hasn't smelled us yet.*

Us?

You.

You saying I stink?

No. I'm saying you smell delicious. I've told you that before.

I still blushed. *So, what do we do?*

Well, if they're both in here, you can bet your ass you picked the right door. They have to be guarding Fenrir.

Shit. You're right.

Now, the question is, are they going to leave anytime soon?

That is literally a god and your mother. Surely, they have better things to do than hang around the body of a sleeping god.

Of course, they do. Makes you wonder what else is guarding it.

I have a plan!

Oh, fuck me. Rome shook his head and rubbed his face.

You might have had a shot, but that was kind of mean, so now I changed my mind.

What's your plan?

Nope. I had one *feel bad left, and you just stomped all over it with your anti-Kaede remarks.*

Kaede... He paused to take a deep, yet quiet as to not alert the angry god and parental unit below. *I'm sorry. What is your brilliant plan?*

Kiss me.

Your brilliant plan is for me to kiss you?

No. Kiss me, and I'll tell you my brilliant plan. I don't know why I said it, but I did. Strike that. I loved teasing Rome. That's why I said it. He was irresistible when he was flustered, and the fastest way to fluster him was to tease him. Besides, I didn't think he had it in him.

I was wrong. His lips found mine, and his tongue parted them before I even registered that he was, in fact, kissing me. But then my brain melted, my toes curled, and the butterflies started flapping in my stomach. That was a pretty good clue.

What's your plan? He didn't wait until the kiss ended to ask. How he could think while I was kissing him was kind of disappointing. So, I slid a hand down to his ass and grabbed a cheek. He inhaled deeply through is nose. Finally, I pulled away. *Look across the cavern. Two levels down, there is another passageway.*

He shook his head and looked across the way. *I see it. How is that going to help us?*

I'm going to sneak around to there, go down that corridor, and turn off the necklace. Then, I'm going to run like my life depends on it while the rest of you get your cute little butts down into that hole and find Fenrir. See? Brilliant.

That's the dumbest fucking idea I've ever heard.

What? Why?

What good is it going to do us to find him, when it has to be you that kills him?

237

Uh… I'm going to keep this stone in my hand. When you find him, I'll double back around and come find you guys.

You know the necklace only stops people from listening in telepathically to conversation and sensing you. You can still be seen, smelled, and most likely heard.

I can be quiet.

He laughed. Out loud. I gave him a shushing motion, and he looked over the edge of the spiral staircase. Sitting very still for a moment, he finally relaxed. *It's too risky.*

Do you have a better plan?

No. But that doesn't mean there isn't one.

It's my call. Get ready to look for Fenrir.

He nodded. With an inaudible sigh, he pulled the heavy chain from his neck and put it over my head. I shifted into my full fox-wolf form and headed down the path, padding as silently as I could and sticking to the wall. Even if they heard me, they wouldn't be able to see me from the angle they were at.

You're doing good. They still don't see or sense you.

Good. I'm halfway there…

Still good. Stop!

I froze mid-step. Hearing their voices below, I lowered myself to the ground and readied my invisibility spell, just in case.

You're good. Keep going.

Lifting myself from my belly, I continued toward the other passage and finally breathed a sigh of relief as I bound through the exit.

I'm in.

Let me know before you trigger the necklace.

I will, as soon as I find a place to hide.

Heading down the dark corridor, I let my eyes shift back to the darkness. It seemed to go on forever until I found a stairwell leading down off the left side of the passage. To the right, another stair led upward. I wanted down and stepped onto the landing, looking over the ledge into darkness. Hopefully it ended on the level they were on. *Hopefully*.

I'm ready.

I'll let you know if they take the bait.

Rome?

Yeah?

Why do you think your mother is here?

She was probably called back by the goddess to guard Fenrir's body. That's the only reason I can think of.

Makes sense. Thanks for answering. It bothered me that Tatsuo knew she was gone, but they were guarding his spirit in the mortal realm. It made sense they would guard his body in Helheim. Just would have been nice to know.

I shifted back into my demi-form and keyed the sequence on the necklace.

They're coming! His mental shout was microseconds before the growl that echoed down the corridor and up from the stairwell. At least I was certain where it went.

Which way?

Up toward us!

Perfect, I thought to myself. I waited until I heard clamoring up the stairs at the end of the passage I'd just traversed. Moments before they hit the landing, I rekeyed the necklace and ran down the stairs as fast as my little feet could propel me.

Found another corridor!

Take it! You'll see a stairway on your left. I should be coming out of it...now!

I collided into Rome.

"Run!" There was no more time for stealth, and I took off in the opposite direction they came, hoping we got to Fenrir *long* before they caught up to us.

We ran for what felt like an eternity. I was huffing and puffing when Rome finally scooped me up and threw me over his shoulder, shifting into his hellhound form.

The corridor whisked by as I held on for dear life.

He skidded to a stop just before we plunged over *another* drop off. He leaned over the edge, and I leaned over his head and whistled.

It went down for *miles.*

"What the fuck? They dig a hole into the center of the earth and toss him down there?"

Rome nodded his gigantic head.

"Legend has it he is suspended on a stone circle, chained to four boulders," Roki hissed from atop Remy.

"How do we get down there?"

Remy shifted, and Roki jumped to the ground before he fell there. "I don't think we can. There aren't any stairs. Kaede, are you *sure* he's down there?"

I nodded, knowing without a doubt he was.

"We can get you down there." Fress looked at his lover who nodded. They shifted and motioned to the chariot behind them.

"Good thing we brought them with us," I said and climbed aboard. Roki and the Romies climbed on behind me.

"Are you sure we can trust them?" Roki was worried because of my prophesy. We didn't have any other choice. It was either that, jump, or face Hel. The kitties seemed like the best choice.

"They brought us here."

"That is what worries me."

The chariot lurched forward, and they leapt from the ledge. We were in free fall for a moment until they started running through the air, circling around the cylindrical cavern and heading downward.

"Merry Christmas to all, and to all, a good night," I shouted and grinned as my voice echoed back at me.

Rome swatted me in the back of the head.

"Oh, stop. It's not like they don't know we are here."

There was a roar from one of the kitties, and I looked over the front of the chariot, my heart freezing mid-beat and icy fear running up my spine.

"There he is."

About a hundred feet below us was the stone disk suspended by magic in the middle of the hole we were flying down. He was spread eagle on his stomach, each one of his paws being pulled taut in the four cardinal directions as Gleipnir coiled around him tethering him to the boulders we couldn't see.

A loud snarl sounded somewhere up above us.

"Stop!" The scream from the goddess above us threatened to deafen everyone. Even the kitties shuddered, the chariot jostling its passengers.

"We're not going to make it!" Rome looked above us, the falling form of the goddess Hel proving his point.

"Yes, I am," I said softly and rolled over the side of the chariot like a deep-sea diver.

Ignoring the three of them screaming my name, I focused on the disk below me. I made a series of pops to slow my descent, not wanting to splatter across the stone disk. The last one put me right above Fenrir, and as I fell, I called my katana…

The blade struck him solidly in his back, just below his massive neck. I felt like a toothpick skewering a whale, that was the size difference between us. At the very last moment, the blade shifted and struck the ropes coiled around him.

Gleipnir screamed, and I watched in horror as I smacked against the freezing gray fur of the wolf god of Ragnarok. The corded blackness began to sizzle and

241

dissolve around my blade. In a moment, the strand frayed and pulled apart. It was like I lit a fuse in the middle, and I watched in rapt horror as the disintegration spread around the torso of the wolf. Wherever it touched, it spread to other coils and eventually headed down the legs of the massive wolf.

When it reached the end, the remaining ropes slithered over the edge of the disk, the boulders crashing against each other and the walls of the cylindrical cavern.

"What have I done?"

"Freed me," Fenrir rumbled.

The chariot landed a moment before the goddess. She dropped the hellhound next to her, who shifted into a frightened looking Headmistress Lateran.

"Foolish child! What have you done?"

I looked at the two of them, standing there and quivering. "I think I done fucked up."

Hel snarled and started forward, but the paw closest to her slid across the stone and positioned itself under the wolf. Then the other front one did the same, and the two hind legs moved at the same time. With a heave, Fenrir's body stood. I popped off his back before I was tossed into the pit below.

He sat and looked down at all of us.

"How?" I probably *shouldn't* have asked, but I did.

His massive head leaned over, and he touched his nose to mine, dead eyes staring at me the whole time. The effect was morbidly creepy. "I knew you would never free me, so I had an accomplice help me."

"Freya…"

He chuckled, the rumbling in his chest shaking the whole disk.

"Freya? Fenrir! What have you done?" Hel seemed just as confused as we were.

"Hello, sister."

242

"Our mistress would never aid the likes of you, cur. Tell us another lie," Fress shouted angrily.

His chuckle became outright laughter, his shoulders bobbing in mirth. "Come out…*Freya.*"

There was a shimmering next to him, and the goddess of love stepped out from behind him, walking sheepishly toward us. The kitties bowed low.

"Mistress…we do not understand…"

Freya shifted, her golden dress sizzling as it melted away. Her hair shortened, and her muscles thickened. He looked exactly like Freya, but a man.

"Freyr," I said in shock.

"Not as dumb as you sound, Little Fox!"

"Who?" The twins asked in unison.

Freyr bowed low, a sweeping gesture full of mirth.

"Freya's twin. One of the Vanir, like her."

"One who wishes to be rid of his ties to the Aesir. The only way to do that was their destruction."

"So, you pretended to be her and concocted the whole ruse about killing him."

"I am still shocked you would try to end me, Little Fox. You should have known better," Fenrir grumbled.

I cowered a little and moved away.

"Fear not. You are not the first mortal to be tricked by a god. Nor will you be the last. Assuming any of them survive."

"Fenrir!" Hel hissed his name.

"What, sister? Are you going to subdue me? Even my shell can best the likes of you." He swiped at her with a paw, lurching across the disk and threatening to spill us all over the edge.

"Kaede, we need to go. Let them fight it out." Rome pulled me from my spot beside the wolf.

"Where is our master? Where is Freya?" The kitties only had eyes for Freyr.

He gave them a smirk. "Safe for now, bound in her hall with a length of Gleipnir loaned from my good friend here." He patted Fenrir.

He had placed too much faith in the bargain he had struck with the god of destruction. Without a thought, Fenrir snapped his jaws over the upper half of the god with a sickening crunch and then launched his body at the wall of the cavern. With a *splat*, he hung there motionless, shock and pain overwhelming him, before he slid for a moment and then freefell into the nothingness below.

"Dumbass," I said with a sigh.

"Quite," Fenrir agreed.

"You gonna kill me, too?" Again, I probably shouldn't have asked...

"Free the cunning little fox who freed me? Perish the thought. You and your friends may go, you have yet to unbind my spirit in your mortal realm. Do so, and you will all live. No more games, Kaede. You are mine. My will is yours. Do as I command."

"Sure thing, Boss." I motioned the guys to the other end of the disk. Fress and Kottr shifted, eager to find their mistress. If my blade could cut through Gleipnir, I would free her. It was the least I could do.

"Kaede," Fenrir rumbled my name once more.

"Yes?"

"Do not plot against me, nor disobey me, again."

"I won't."

He nodded. "I shall lie in wait here until my spirit is free. Do not dawdle."

Nodding once again, I climbed into the chariot. Frantic to get the hell out of Hellheim. Away from *him*.

The four of us gripped the chariot, and we were off, winding around the walls of the cavern and going up, and up, and up. We spilled out of the mouth of the smoking volcano.

Epilogue

My tears made viewing David's body upon the unlit pyre nearly impossible. He was covered in a black shroud, but I knew it was him. I could feel it. Even passed on, I could feel him. This was truly the end. The last time I would have my heart broken as he was taken from me.

The funeral was supposed to have been days ago, but Uncle had postponed time and time again, until matters were settled and I could handle it emotionally. I thought it was a hundred years too early, but when I complained, Uncle gave me a sad smile.

We stood, the four of us, David's pack, by his body. Rome was on my left, Remy my right, and Roki behind me. They surrounded me, supported me, and loved me, even though they were hurting just as bad as I was. Not one of us had a dry eye. Even Rome sobbed as Fress and Kottr bore the body to the pyre.

The rest of the school stood behind us, to bear witness and pay their last respects to their fellow student. Everyone but Geri. When she had found out what Steph had done, she vowed to all of us she would return with her, or her body. For the first time since she'd been bound to me, I trusted her.

Lornca and her mate, who was just as shocked as the Kitties to find out Freya wasn't Freya, led Uncle to the front, on the opposite side of David from us. The elves began singing, and the words and melody pulled some of the pain from my heart with its beauty. You could almost feel the song guiding David's body to its final rest. They sang for what felt like days, but was over in a minute, and as the last note touched our ears, the sun crested the horizon, plunging the rocky beach on the coast into darkness.

Tatsuo, shifted. It had been quite a while since I'd seen him in his full draconic form. He craned his neck over David's body, and I reached up to run my hand over his snout like I had done so many times as a child. The huff off his warm breath even made me smile.

He stepped back and motioned for us to do the same. When we were clear, he raised his head to the sky, roared, and then spewed fire at David's pyre. The heat practically blistered our skin, but we didn't move. Couldn't tear our eyes from our friend and love until his body was nothing but ash.

Tatsuo shifted back, bowed his head at us, and left. The elves opened an obsidian jar and sang once again. The ashes that remained swirled up into the air and into the jar. When it was over, they closed the lid and walked it over to the four of us.

"I am sure he would wish to be with you. Keep him with you, or find him a spot for his eternal rest. He is yours, just as he always was."

Fucking elves. They made me cry even more.

∞ ∞ ∞

"Hel is dead."

I sat in the chair in front of Tatsuo's desk. A battered, broken, very tired looking Headmistress Lateran standing beside an equally tired looking Tatsuo.

"Like, dead-dead, or mostly dead?"

246

"This is not the time for jokes, Kaede. You have freed Fenrir's body," Uncle said sadly.

"Well, I didn't know! I mean for fuck's sake…these gods play games like chess masters. I know one thing… It will be over my dead fucking body before I release his spirit."

I still had the necklace on. It was the only way to keep him out of my head. When we got back to the school, I'd shut it down and been barraged by commands to go free his spirt. By the time I turned it back on, my ears and nose were bleeding, and that wasn't an exaggeration. I spent an hour in a very remorseful Lornca's infirmary before the headache finally dulled down to a roar.

"Fenrir did to Hel what he did to Freyr. If they live, it will be a millennium before they heal enough to crawl from their prison," Lateran said angrily.

"Forgive me if I hope they don't make it."

Lateran snarled and lunged, but Tatsuo stopped her with an outstretched hand. "You can hardly blame the child, Isabella. Hel tried to murder her through your daughter's hand."

"Another matter for which this creature will pay!"

Ever seen a pissed off dragon? Even in human form? Scary doesn't even begin to describe it. He surged from his chair, and the room filled with the shadows of his invisible wings as he stared down at his hellhound assistant headmaster. She cowered and actually held her arms over her head.

"She escaped from prison, made multiple attempts on my niece's life, killed her classmate…and you have the presumption to tell me that you seek retribution?" His voice boomed through the room, over the school, and could possibly be heard in Oddi, maybe even Reykjavik.

"No." She sobbed, kneeling on the floor. "Even though Hel commanded her death, my daughter let her own

247

insecurities fester, and her heart became tainted. I do not hold the creature responsible."

"That creature is the lover of your two remaining children and pack. I suggest you treat her with the respect that she deserves."

"Deserves? She has been instrumental in bringing about Ragnarok."

"Would you have fared any different with the subterfuge of the gods?"

She thought about it for a moment before shaking her head. "No. Even Hel was convinced that Freya was who she claimed to be."

"Then this is the last we will hear about it. We need to figure out a way to destroy Fenrir's spirit. That is the only way."

"Agreed."

I just nodded. While my uncle was scary as fuck, I was enjoying the little show. Mostly because it wasn't directed at me. I had to fight the urge to cheer mid rant. He definitely deserved a hug for all that.

"What if we unbind her?"

"The chain cannot be broken, Isabella."

"That is what we thought. She has already freed Freya. Her sword pierced through it like a hot knife through butter. Maybe she can do it to the chains that bind *her*?"

"Not without sacrificing herself upon her sword, I'm afraid."

Lateran seemed a little too pleased with *that* outcome, until Tatsuo narrowed his eyes at her. "I am sure we can come up with something. She is a resourceful girl."

I blinked in shock. That was the first compliment the woman had ever given me.

"We will need help."

"From whom?"

"The gods if need be. This affects them just as much as us. At least Kaede has a voice." He nodded at me, referring to the debt the real Freya owed one little foxlike immortal mortal. Me.

She was *very* grateful when I cut her off the tendril of Gleipnir her brother had bound her in. She cried a few dozen ounces of golden tears and gifted them to me, as well as my new feline guards and chauffeurs. As long as I didn't mind freezing my ass off riding in the back of a chariot in Iceland in winter. They saved us a bunch in gold coins, though. I wasn't mad at her at all, even a little. It had been her brother the whole time since I'd first been stabbed.

"We shall see," Lateran said with a *humph*.

"That is all, Kaede," Uncle said dismissively. He knew I had a hot date planned for the evening. I deserved it. No gods, no school, no nothing but a good time.

"Thanks, Headmaster." I knew better than to call him Uncle in front of Lateran.

He nodded, and I left them standing there, briefly wondering again if anything was going on between the two of them other than school administration. I hated to admit it, because she acted like a crone, but she wasn't bad looking. For a dog.

"You ready?"

I jumped four feet in the air and landed with my hackles raised. "Fuckballs, Rome. You scared the shit out of me."

"We can swing by your room if you want to change your underpants."

"It was an expression." I leaned closer to him. "And who said I was wearing any?" I kissed his cheek and laughed like an evil genius when he sputtered and turned red.

"Are you?" he called after me. The kitties were waiting for Rome and I at the front of the school. I felt bad for having them wait for us, but I'd been called to the headmaster's office on the way to dinner. It was Rome's and my *first official* date. Kind of felt bad for him, too.

"I don't remember if I put any on or not… Maybe you'll find out."

He growled in frustration behind me. It was going to be a fun night.

"You sure you want to do this?"

"Do what?"

"Date me. I'm kind of high maintenance."

His hand on my arm stopped me from taking another step. Especially when he spun me to face him. "I've never been more sure of anything." He leaned over and kissed me. No heavy tongue dueling kissing, just a firm press of our mouths, followed by a hand sliding up my back. I whimpered from the heat of it.

He was most definitely maybe finding out if I was wearing underwear later.

∞ ∞ ∞

"Oh, my *kami*, I'm friggin' full." I lay back in the plastic bench covered in simulated wood grain and rubbed my tummy.

"Too full to dance?"

"Never too full for that. Want the rest of my cheekin?" I shoved my bucket toward him. There were only two wings left, but he still looked a little hungry. And yes, we went to KFC for our first date. I'm cheap.

"No. I'm full, too. Thank you, though."

I grinned at him.

H-h-help…m-m-meeeee.

I sighed and sat up. "Please tell me you fucking heard that."

"Heard what?"

"Voice in my head asking for help."

"Um… I'm going to go out on a limb and say that it's probably a good thing I can't hear the voices in your head."

"I'm going to go ahead and agree with you. Mind if I'm jealous of you?"

"Be my guest. Have the voices stopped?"

I tilted my head and listened. Nothing. "Yerp."

"Well, it can't be a god or anything. You're still wearing your necklace. It looks much nicer on you now that the headmaster had it shrunk down."

"My back is grateful for that, too."

"Maybe it really was just a voice in your head?"

H-h-help…m-m-meeeee.

"Nope. Just heard it again."

"What does it sound like?"

Sighing again, I answered truthfully. "Your sister."

"Kaede… You have *nothing* to feel guilty about."

"You think it's a Freudian voice in my head?"

"Don't you?"

"Sounds pretty real and bitchy to me."

"My sister is dead, Kaede. It can't be her?"

"Didn't say it *was* her. I said it *sounded* like her."

He sat up and looked at me. I mean *really* looked at me, staring into my eyes for a few moments. "Steph?"

I smashed the top of my almost empty bucket of chicken. "If it *is* her, I'ma kill her. Why can't she go haunt someone else?"

Rome paused to think for a moment. "Because she's not dead…"

"Great. Then where the hell is she?"

"Sabine could create and control the rifts into her pocket dimension… If Steph was in there when you killed Sabine…"

"She's…stuck."

Rome nodded.

251

"Know what?"

"What?"

"Sucks to be her. I'll let Geri know she can call off the search. Come on. Let's go dancing."

He chuckled and got up. Offering me a slightly sticky from chicken hand, he pulled me to my feet and kissed me.

"Mmmm. Chicken kisses…"

Author's Note

Reviews are important for new authors, and I greatly appreciate everyone who takes a moment to leave one, even a line or two! Thank you so much for reading my reverse harem series! I'm writing away, and more books will be out soon!

Follow me on Amazon to be sent updates on my new releases!

Come hang out in my reader's group, Coven of the First Moon, on Facebook! Keep up to date on releases, enjoy loads of teasers on works in progress, and special alternate POV's! Oh, and lots of inappropriate things.

Flip the page for my bio and all my other stalking links.

Don't forget to check out my other RH series, Lovin' the Coven!

About the Author

A late comer to the writing game, Jacquelyn had always been a fan of romance novels and lately become addicted to the reverse harem category. I mean seriously, who wouldn't? Sitting alone one night she flipped open her laptop and said, "I'm going to give this a whirl." And thus, the Lovin' the Coven series was given life. She has designs on other series as well, but only time shall tell.

As for her, she is five-foot-something, with graying hair, wicked eyes, an eager smile, and an annoying laugh. She lives at home with her dog, a cat, and that is about all she is comfortable sharing.

Other Works

Lovin' the Coven Series
(Reverse Harem- 7 book series)

First Moon
Second Blood
Third Charm
Fourth Rite
Fifth Essence
Sixth Sense
Seventh Seal

The Fox and the Hounds
(Reverse Harem – trilogy)

A Tail of Woah
A Tail of Two Kitties
The Tell Tail Heart

Other

Girlfiend (Standalone YA Paranormal Romance)
Succubus Soccer Mom (Reverse Harem Standalone)